Story Institute Presents: Ramblings & Verses

Volume I:
Let Me Not Begin Anew

———————————————

Edited by: John E. Murray, III

Library of Congress Control Number: 2010912595

ISBN-13: 978-0-9794451-3-2 (pbk.)

ISBN-10: 0-9794451-3-2 (pbk.)

A Story Institute Publication
www.storyinstitute.com

To the inspiration inside all of us...

TABLE OF CONTENTS

INTRODUCTION 1

ENGAGING THE BEAST OF BELIEF 6

SHORT STORIES
BELIEVE IN YOUR STORIES

LITTLE 7

KAYLEE'S QUARTER 8

THE LADY OF THE FOUNTAIN 16

THE SLOPE OF WAR 19

THE FINAL FORTRESS 27

CHARACTERS LIVE IN STORIES

WRITING THROUGH THE WORDS TO YOUR CHARACTERS... 32

EACH 33

ALIVE 34

THE DARKNESS OF PAST 44

GROW YOUR STORIES

ENGAGE A NEW OUTLOOK... 60

BABBLING FOR... 61

TOO LOW FOR DINNER 62

HONESTY IS 67

HOME SWEET HOME 72

TABLE OF CONTENTS

POEMS

EXPERIENCE INSIDE VERSES

SEARCH FOR A SUBJECT... 92

EARLY MORNINGS...93

COLE RIDGE POEM 94

CORE...95

WATCH 96

LEMON 97

THE COLLAPSE OF SUMMER...98

SELECTED POEMS 99

THE FIFTY THINGS WRONG WITH THIS PICTURE 100

BITTER AWARENESS..101

MOVING ON 102

SICKNESS..103

I FORGET...IS IT NAPTIME?...104

INSPIRED WITHIN VERSES

PRAISE YOUR MUSE... 106

WONDROUS HAPPINESS 107

THE NIGHT WAS MADE FOR ROMANCE 108

OUR LOVE..108

ONLY LOVE..108

MY LOVER, MY FRIEND 109

SO LOST...110

WHO ARE YOU? 111

TABLE OF CONTENTS

PERFECT MAN 112

READ, THEN WRITE... 114

IT IS A LONG...LONG...LONG DAY... 115

THE MACHINE: TIME DRIVEN 116

AD FINEM 117

INTERPRETATIONS 118

HOLOCAUST 120

FOR WHAT I KNOW 121

CHANGING TIMES 122

REACHING INTO YOUR VERSES

FIND YOUR TIME AND WRITE... 124

WANTING TO BECOME ME 125

AN ENDING OF A SIMILAR KIND 126

SHIP OF GOLD 127

THE LOVE YOU SHARE 128

A NEWBORN CHILD 129

SNOWFLAKE 130

OPEN RANGE 132

LIVE, LAUGH, LOVE 134

THE CHRISTMAS ANGEL 135

THE PEARL 136

BREAST CANCER SURVIVOR'S PRAYER 138

GOOD MORNING 139

TIMELESS TALES... 140

Introduction

Whether you are composing a poem, scribbling a short story, or scratching out a novel, an inspiration is needed to get you going and maintain the explosions of creativity throughout your piece. Sometimes, we wonder where to find our missing muse. Sometimes, we think we see them, but become tricked by the lure of another voice. You may even consider venturing out on a mental walk-about to find your connect. No matter what method you use, as a writer, you know that you need to find the inspiration before continuing. Otherwise, your verses, stories, and endeavors will become random ramblings lost without a muse...

Muses can be found in the strangest of places...under an old pile of clothes...around buildings...under your desk...behind the eyes of a new friend...in the mirror...or, in your left pocket...in fact, you had better check your pocket now...go ahead...we'll wait...

You didn't really check did you...oh well, maybe someone else will find that one...

The writers, authors, and poets within this volume of Story Institute Presents: Ramblings and Verses may have even found the one you ignored. We hope you enjoy reading each and encourage you to use the inspirations you recognize to create your own storylines.

Visit us at www.storyinstitute.com to read, hear, and explore more...in the meantime, remember to Imagine, Enhance, and Grow your stories!

<u>Let Me Not Begin Anew</u>

Let me not begin anew.
Let me spend my days with you, or you, or you,
My friends, my companions, my creations.
Losing you would be a great devastation.
You are my entire being,
The results of my dreaming.
With every word I breathe,
You are able to achieve
New invigorating life
To help me deal with all the strife.
I need, I want, I feel,
Only what I believe real.
That being you
To whom I will always remain true.
So, go forth
And let your intensity be shown.
For with you,
I will never be alone.

John E. Murray, III

SHORT STORIES

BELIEVE

IN YOUR

STORIES

Engaging the Beast of Belief

So, you have invested much time in coming up with the plot, character names, and even the house that your grandfather, Jack, built. You begin writing. You get through page 1, move to page 2, and reach page 3, when that moment hits...the moment, during a normal dream when your characters are sitting in the corner booth at the local diner and look up at you. They proceed to have a conversation with you on their past, their future, and ask to be written out of the scene that you left them in for the last month. If you reach this point, you have stared into the beast of belief and entered the conquering stage. Once you start to believe, engage yourself in the storyline. Bring your thoughts and passion back to the ramblings. Your characters and readers will thank you.

Children are the greatest source of belief. They not only make up good, simple stories, but they believe them. They believe in their imagination so much, it is difficult to avoid being pulled in yourself. When you are within the inner confines of belief, stay there for a while and watch the children. Watch how they play and interact with their imagination. Watch and listen to the conversations they have in their own little world. Then, step back a little. Watch other people interact with each other. When you return to your writing share what you observed with your characters and continually breathe life into your story. Shake the trees just enough so that some of those beliefs fall and become replanted in the minds of your readers.

The writing in this section includes some award-winning prose that connects to a sense of belief. Listen to the voices as you read and allow yourself to open up the possibilities...

Little

A little piece of dirt,
I see you, dried up in the scorching sun,
Waiting for a drop of rain,
To soak away the cracks and pain.

A little piece of land,
With dirt and bugs a little bland,
No vegetation growing in this earth,
I wonder what it's worth.

A little piece of me,
Deserted from the life I know,
Is this the way I want to live,
No experiences to help me grow.

Moisture for the dirt,
Water for the land,
Emotion for my life,
And the will to take a stand.

All the little pieces,
Are essential for the whole,
All the little life experiences,
Are essential for your soul.

Give yourself a little dream,
Take a little glance,
At the life you've left out to dry,
Give it another chance.

Skyler Wolf Jones

Kaylee's Quarter

Rebecca Laskowitz

Kaylee grasped her mother's hand as they made their way up the icy stone walkway. Snow covered the edge of the path where flowers usually blossomed during the spring. She watched her step so as not to fall and ruin her new pink puffy coat. It was her first Christmas present of the year from her parents. Even though Christmas Eve wasn't until tomorrow night, the frigid weather allowed for Kaylee to receive her coat a few days early.

While one gloved hand clung desperately to her mother, the other held just as tightly onto Bunny. Bunny went everywhere with Kaylee since she was two. The stuffed rabbit's ears were tattered from months of teething, and his yellow coloring faded from hundreds of journeys through the washing machine. Kaylee held him by the ears and raised her arm just high enough to keep his fluffy bottom from dragging on the cold, wet ground.

After making her way up the front steps, Kaylee turned around to watch her father carry their bags. Her Hello Kitty duffle bag stood out against her parents' gray luggage. She wondered why grownups chose such boring colors.

Kaylee spun around at the sound of the front door opening. Her grandmother's face had her usual smile stretching from ear to ear. Kaylee loved her grandmother's smile. It was always sincere and her teeth were the brightest shade of white.

"Hi, dearies," she exclaimed as she stepped aside to let her children enter the warm house. The smell of apple pie and sweet potatoes filled Kaylee's nostrils the instant she crossed the threshold. Holiday spirit was palpable in her grandparents' house.

As her grandmother leaned down to take off her coat, Kaylee's grip on Bunny remained firm.

"What a beautiful coat, Kaylee," Grandma said. "Where did you get it?"

"Mommy and Daddy gave it to me for Christmas," she replied softly. The sounds of chatter coming from the other room kept Kaylee glued to her spot in the foyer. It usually took her a while to ease out of her shyness.

"A new coat for Christmas!" Kaylee jumped at the bellowing voice of her grandfather. "What a lucky girl, getting her presents early." He scooped her up in a big bear hug and planted a kiss on her that smushed her cheeks together. "Want to go say hi to everyone?"

Before she could say no, she was being carried into the next room. The sight of so many people caused Kaylee to bury her face in her grandfather's sweater.

"Aw, look who's being shy," sang her aunt's familiar birdlike voice. Kaylee felt long, fake nails tickle her neck. She shrugged her shoulders to protect her neck from the invading fingers. "I have something you, sweetie." Kaylee peeked out from her grandfather's shoulder and saw a Hershey Kiss in her aunt's outstretched hand. She reached out her tiny hand to grab the candy, but before she could claim it, her aunt's fingers closed around it. "First and hug, then you get the kiss."

Kaylee hesitated, but the thought of chocolate helped her conquer her bashfulness. She held out her arms, Bunny still dangling from her right hand, and wrapped them around her aunt's neck. She was embraced in another bear hug and received a glossy kiss on her cheek before being set down. As soon as she had her chocolate, Kaylee turned and ventured further into the crowded room. She didn't make eye contact with anyone, and her answers to everyone's questions were short.

"How are you?" "Good."

"Who's in your hand?" "Bunny."

"How old are you?" "Five."

"Are you excited for Santa?" "Yes."

Kaylee finally found her way to the other side of the room. She sat in her little seat positioned next to the Christmas tree. From here she could observe her bustling relatives catching up after being separated for months by hundreds of miles. Kaylee enjoyed watching people and listening in on their conversations. Especially when she was the topic of the conversations. People often made comments about her thinking she couldn't hear them.

"She's gotten so big!"

"She has her father's nose."

"And her mother's brown hair."

"But where did the curls come from?"

"She's too skinny."

As Kaylee sat listening to the grownups around her, a loud greeting was heard in the foyer. She wondered who had arrived that warranted such an uproarious welcome. Her mother walked into the room and announced that Granddad had arrived.

Kaylee stiffened in her seat. She knew that her mother's grandfather was her Great Grandfather Henry. Before anyone noticed her moving, Kaylee escaped out of the other door in the room and into the kitchen, dragging Bunny on the floor behind her. Her heart pounded with fear when she though of Great Grandpa Henry. His frail ninety-five year old frame crept slowly forward with the support of his cane as his third leg. His tired face seemed to have permanently wrinkled up into a frown. His eyes were sunken in and gloomy. Kaylee was sure she would turn to stone whenever she looked into the two pits of darkness on his face.

When dinnertime came around, Kaylee was relieved to be placed between her parents. Great Grandpa Henry, as the oldest member of the family, was perched at the head of the long table. His food was served to him while everyone else served themselves. He barely spoke—just gave slight nods when her mother or aunt pointed to the various serving plates. His movements were slow and stiff. It often pained Kaylee to watch him exert any kind of energy.

When he chewed his food, his jaw moved just as slowly as the rest of his body. His teeth always looked like they were going to fall out. Everything about him frightened Kaylee. While everyone else treated him with love and respect, Kaylee did her best to hide from him. She saw her great grandfather as a scary monster, slinking slowly through the hallways, making creepy wheezing sounds when he breathed, walking hunched over like he was preparing to attack any little creature that got in his way. To Kaylee, there was nothing great or grand or fatherly about Henry.

By nine o'clock, Kaylee had made it through the evening of staring and coddling from her aunts and uncles and was tucked into bed. Her father gave her a kiss on the forehead.

"Can you tell me a story?" asked Kaylee as her father stood up.

"Not tonight, sweetie. I'm gonna go talk with people downstairs. It's been a long time since we've seen everyone."

"Please," implored Kaylee with a pleading look in her eyes. Kaylee always took advantage of her father's weakness for her big brown eyes.

"Sorry, but not tonight. I'll tell you two tomorrow night. How does that sound?"

Kaylee hesitated before accepting the offer. Her father left her alone in the room, leaving the door slightly ajar. She closed her eyes after making sure Bunny was securely at her side.

She was just about the drift off to sleep when she hear footsteps in the hallway. Her excitement grew as she expected her father to come back and tell her a story after all. But just as quickly as her excitement grew, it dissipated when she realized the footsteps didn't belong to her father. They sounded much too slow, and if she wasn't mistaken, the person had three feet instead of two.

Before she could figure out who was coming, a shadow filled the crack in the door. Kaylee sat up and clutched Bunny to her chest. A slight creek sounded as the door slowly opened. As the crack in the door widened, so did Kaylee's eyes. Her pulse quickened and her skin went cold as Great Grandpa Henry took shape in the door frame.

When the door was completely open, Henry slowly made his way into the room. Time seemed to slow down as he made his way towards her bed. Kaylee sat perfectly still, too afraid to move. Bunny was locked in a death grip between Kaylee's arms, chest and chin. After seconds that felt like hours, Henry hovered over the bed leaning heavily on his cane. His sunken eyes stared down at her like two pieces of coal. And then, just when she thought he couldn't inch any closer, his free hand reached out to her, wrinkled and trembling.

Kaylee ducked her head as far as she could, but the hand continued to creep towards her. She shuddered when she felt Henry's cool skin brush past her cheek and reach behind her ear. Kaylee's mouth opened slightly and a whimpering sound escaped her lips. The whimper was about to turn into a scream when the hand returned from behind her ear. Kaylee's anxiety turned to amazement when Great Grandpa Henry held a shiny quarter in front of her eyes. Her hand shot up to her ear and her mouth dropped open.

Henry smiled. "I saw something shiny behind your ear during dinner." He held the quarter out to her. After a slight hesitation, Kaylee reached out and accepted the gift. "Do you like bedtime stories?" he asked softly.

Kaylee couldn't hide her excitement as her eyes lit up. "Yes," she replied meekly and leaned back against her pillow.

Henry turned around and sat on the side of the bed. Kaylee bent her legs to give the elderly man more room.

"Once upon a time, in a land across the sea, there lived a young magician known far and wide. Audiences traveled hundreds of miles to see Haunting Henry perform his legendary disappearing acts. His fame allowed him to travel to many countries, including America where he eventually met his future wife."

Kaylee listened with fascination as her great grandfather detailed his journey from being a young boy with a desire to be different and amazing to an internationally acclaimed illusionist.

By the time the story came to an end, Kaylee was sitting on the edge of her bed looking up at Great Grandpa Henry with curiosity. Henry noticed her questioning gaze and smiled.
"Is there anything you want to know?" he asked as he put his arm around her lovingly.

Kaylee stared down at her palm where the quarter still rested. "When did you learn the quarter trick?"

"When I was five years old," he whispered.

"Like me?" Kaylee responded excitedly.

"Like you." Henry leaned over and gave Kaylee a kiss on the cheek. Then, with the support of the nightstand and his third leg, he rose and began his slow journey out of the room. As he reached the door, Kaylee sat up quickly.

"Great Grandpa?"

"Yes, dear?"

"What was the best magic you ever did?"

"My family." His response came without hesitation. "I created my family."

The Lady of the Fountain

Amy Priddy

George woke up that morning with a splitting headache and found himself in a whirlwind of confusion. He rubbed his eyes and seemed to glare back at the sunlight pouring through the shutters. George hated the sunlight and almost everything else that morning entailed. He flopped out of bed, put on a worn out blue robe and tied it around his sagging midsection. After his wife died he had promised himself that he would work on his appearance, but the thought of actual work made him queasy. He went to the mirror and frowned at the wrinkles around his eyes and meticulously tried to rub them away with his finger. It didn't work, of course, and his face continued to hang there lifelessly.

The chirping of the morning birds woke him from his trance and his bottled up anger started to boil within his body. Those damn birds, he thought. I hate them. Not everyone in the world likes to hear the sweet chirping of birds in the morning. His face reddened in anger at the sound of their perfect melodies and he turned to throw a shoe at the open window. George's hand quickly fell toward the ground, his eyes opening wide in fear as he caught the glimpse of a shadow out of the corner of his eye. The shadows quickly gathered in the room, pushing the older man to a corner where he shook in fear. He remembered his walk by the park the night before and the fun he had throwing pennies into a fountain with a little boy. The boy told him to make a wish, but the man didn't listen and upset the woman spirit that lived within the statue of the fountain. The boy grew very upset with him and viciously pointed his finger at the old man, threatening him.

"You didn't make a wish? Why would you do that?" the boy questioned.

"Son, it's just pretend. This isn't real and she isn't real," George said as he pointed to the lifeless statue.

"Just wait! You'll see!" the boy shouted as he ran down the street. "She'll make you pay for not believin' in her!"

George's mind fluttered back to his bedroom that had been taken over by spirits and he quickly panicked. He started throwing all his dirty laundry at the shadows, but this made them only grow in numbers. The spirits screeched at the man and clawed at the light that was within the room. This was their Hell and they wanted back into their darkness. A sound echoed within the room, like the call of their leader, and the ghosts retreated back to their world. George sighed with relief. They were gone.

He thought about the words from the little boy and decided to venture back to the fountain in the park. The sun disappeared and darkness filled the sky; not from the clouds, but from the demons that now appeared. He couldn't escape them and grew frightened from this new world that the spirit had cursed him with. He ran in terror passed ghosts and monsters and demons hiding in the alleys. The werewolves howled at the moonlight and licked their sharp fangs that desired the rip of flesh and taste of blood. They ran after him and he could feel their hot breath upon his neck. Closer and closer they pursued him, but soon vanished as he came upon the fountain in the middle of the park. George leaned against the statue as he tried to catch his breath. The water in the bottom of the fountain was turning green and smelled stale with age. Her paint was chipping and she no longer held the luster that she had so many years ago. He tried to forget about the demons that surrounded his life and held the statue that night as if she was real. He was alone and the statue was the only thing that seemed real to him. She protected him from the terrors of the night.

The statue was made in his wife's honor and all the sick children she had helped when she was a nurse. She was their savior, so the city had a statue of his wife placed in the park where she could watch the children play. George stopped visiting her over the years and his sadness grew into hatred and self-pity. He hated her for leaving him and never accepted being alone. Tears welled up in his eyes as he knelt done and polished the brass nameplate with his thumb. Oh, Margaret, he sighed. I'm so sorry that I've disappointed you. I just didn't think life would be this hard without you. He moved in closer to the statue of the woman, placed his moistened face upon her breast, and then he was gone.

The boy came by again that night to pay his respects to the woman that saved his life, but he was shocked to find the display that was in front of him. The statue had grown in size and now took on the shape of a man and a woman in each other's arms. The boy smiled at the couple and said his thanks to his special nurse. He turned to walk away, but decided to make one final wish. His penny soared through the air and actually landed in the hand of the lady and he smiled with delight.

"I wish..." the boy began. "I wish that you're both finally happy."

The Slope of War

Yael K. Miller

He was a scout.

He could have been an officer but he made his choice years ago. He had no interest in being an officer and his job as a scout kept him as far away from officers as possible and for a majority of the time. He had been in this business for a great many years as evident from the braid and stripes on the underarms of his Blue uniform.

Years ago, long before his birth, it was decided that ranking should not be so visible. It could be seen now only if a person stood right in front of another person and even then you could still prevent people from seeing the ranking. It was a good system and he enjoyed the rare occasions when he got to flash his underarms. This was one of those times.

He had been called to the Blue command tent. As he entered the camp he saw how few of them had survived. He could see the aftermath of a very recent battle. A defeat no doubt. He, of course, had been somewhere else scouting. He followed the discreet signs to the command tent – an old code that had never been broken. Or so he assumed as he had never heard otherwise and never heard about a command tent being specifically attacked.

He flashed his rank markings and gave his name to the guard outside the command tent. The guard had just passed the enthusiasm of youth and had not yet settled into the comfort of veteranhood.

"What happened?" the scout asked.

At this the guard got suspicious and lightly touched his belted pistol.

The scout again flashed his rank markings. "I'm a scout."

The guard relaxed. "I'm probably not suppose to say this but the Maroon boys ground us into little bits."

The scout nodded. He had seen the effects in the camp.

"The command tent's been reviewing the whole battle for the last two days," the guard said, "discussing some Maroon master strategist." The guard described in great detail the battle; he had been in the fight and had also eavesdropped at his post for the last two days.

The scout started to get an idea why he had been called but did not let his thoughts weigh too heavily. After all, these were officers and, beyond that, command officers. Who knows if they actually lived in the same universe as the rest of the world?

The scout nodded at the guard. The guard called out in a soft firm voice: "Scout Specialist reporting as ordered."

There was a grunt from the command tent that both the scout and the guard interpreted as permission to enter. The guard held open the tent door and the scout entered.

Inside the tent all the command officers clustered around a table covered in maps. Though most of their rank markings were obscured, from what the scout could see and who he recognized from his long career, the scout figured that all of command were huddled in this tent. Apparently, the Maroons really hadn't cracked the code to the location of the command tent.

The scout was handed a picture. "This is the Maroon commander that made us eat dirt," said an old familiar face.

The scout saw the other commanders frowning at the phrase but said nothing. Then he saw the old familiar commander was missing a rank mark. Apparently the other commanders had already spoken their piece. It was nice to see that, in the midst of the aftermath of a crushing defeat, the command structure still had time to place blame and demote.

"Something must be done," said a baby-faced commander, echoed in nods from the rest of the command except the one with whom the scout was familiar. As if a scout had no idea of how a war works.
"A sniper attack should do it," said the old familiar face.

After long experience, the scout had stilled his mental remarks from becoming public: "Are you insane? Sniping an enemy commander, not in battle, and a labeled master strategist? I know, I'll send him a note inviting him for tea."

The other commanders took the scout's silence for stupidity or perhaps cowardice. But the old familiar face knew what it was and grinned. He said to the scout, "This Maroon commander takes walks in a forest clearing just beyond the no-man's land at dusk." The scout was handed a Maroon uniform – a lowly private by the rank markings. "Wear this."

The baby-faced commander gestured the scout to a map. "Here's the defense map of our side of no-man's land and what we know of theirs."

The scout quickly memorized the map: mines, chemical traps, and other nasty stuff. This is what made him such an excellent scout, the ability to quickly assimilate maps and terrain and apply the knowledge to survival.

It was clearly the end of the meeting; the scout waiting to be dismissed and the old familiar face about to open his mouth when one of the baby-faced commander's cohorts said, "This mission is absolutely vital. Failure is not an option. You're dismissed."

As the scout left the tent and nodded to the friendly guard, he could only think that this was further proof that he was glad he had never become an officer. Something about being an officer must fry a person's brains so he can only state the obvious.

Just outside the camp, the scout changed into the Maroon uniform. He belted on a pistol even though it was not standard for a lowly private to carry one; the scout always figured better safe than sorry. The scout removed his sniper rifle from its hiding place and attached all the extensions for an extra long shot.

The scout crept into the no-man's land with heavy fog blanketing the area. He wove his way through the Blue traps of his own side and went as far as he could into the Maroon-trapped area. Lying down in a sniper prone position, he lined up his rifle scope with the forest clearing and waited for dusk.

He was patient, a veteran. Although he much preferred his scout duties, he was no untried greenie as a sniper.

Dusk approached and the fog shifted away from the forest clearing. It looked to be close to perfect conditions for a sniper shot.

And then a figure in Maroon walked into the clearing. The scout could not yet definitely identify that this was his target as the Maroon paced back and forth. Finally the Maroon stopped pacing and sat on a tree stump. Now the scout could confirm that this was his target. The scout waited to ensure that the Maroon was not about to move. The scout lined up the shot just as the Maroon turned his head to the side leaving the scout with only a profile at which to fire. But this was no problem for the scout, and so he pulled the trigger.

At that moment the scout saw something impossible in his scope. The target had turned his head back so that the scout could again see the target's face. The target was no longer the Maroon that he had been shown the picture of but himself, the scout! Somehow he, the scout, sat on that tree stump.

The scout dropped his sniper rifle and sprinted to the forest clearing – praying he'd dodge Maroon traps, running on pure adrenalin, something he had not done since a young, green scout. He made it to the forest clearing just as the bullet hit the target/himself/the person's head. The scout drew his pistol and nudged the body over. The body's face was completely gone – the scout had no clue whether he had impossibly shot himself.

Two Maroon figures dashed into the clearing carrying automatic weapons. The scout was outgunned and did not bother to fire at the Maroon men. The scout only hoped they would be merciful when they figured out he had killed their master strategist commander.

One of the men, hopelessly young and slightly out of breath, said, "Commander, are you alright? We heard a gunshot."

The scout thought: "Are you insane? Your commander is lying on the ground."

The two Maroons were not looking at the body but at him as if he, a Blue scout in a stolen Maroon uniform, were their commander.

Something impossible was going on. The scout drew in a breath and thought: "I guess I'm the commander of these Maroons."

The scout-now-commander said, "A Blue in a stolen Maroon uniform snuck through the no-man's land and tried to kill me."

Only now did the two Maroons look at the body. The other Maroon, a veteran and someone apparently quite familiar with the Maroon commander, said, "I told you, Commander, it's too dangerous for you to be walking in this clearing. I know you said you needed to get away to think but now your safety has been compromised."

The scout-now-commander allowed himself to be herded between the two Maroons into the Maroon camp. It was a healthy camp with few wounded, not like the Blue camp, and, as he walked, he noticed the stiffening of soldiers as he passed – the coming to attention when a well-respected commander walks by. All of these Maroons thought he was a Maroon commander. Flashing his rank markings to himself, he saw they were no longer the markings of a lowly private on the uniform he put on earlier today. They were the markings of a very high-ranking and well-decorated commander.

His two Maroon bodyguards escorted him to what he assumed was the Maroon command tent. On the way he did not recognize the codes to a command tent, although in truth he had not been looking so hard. He entered, and the commanders in the tent all came to attention.

"Clear your head, sir?" one commander said in tones of an subordinate talking to a superior and desperately hoping the superior knows what to do.

He nodded and moved to the table. On it lay maps of incomplete plans of a battle. The same battle that had decimated the Blues two days ago. He now understood what was happening – at least as far as he could. This was a he that had not stayed a scout but had become an officer, a command officer. All the other commanders in the tent looked at him for a plan. What could he do? Just this morning he was a Blue scout. Could he really turn his back on the Blues and plan a Maroon victory? Looking around the tent, he realized he had to do this. Somehow, someway, he had become a Maroon and the Maroons needed him – they were his people now.

He took a deep breath and moved forward. He explained his plan of attack based on what the Blue guard told him about the battle two days ago and the map of the Maroon side of no-man's land he saw earlier. A brilliant plan – the other commanders were in awe. "We strike at two hours before dawn," he said. After all the commanders completely understood the plan, they dispersed to inform their own subordinates.

He laid down to sleep after informing his guards not to wake him, not even during the battle. Although he was now a Maroon commander and the Maroons were his people, he had no desire to see the Blues slaughtered.

He awoke late in the afternoon to murmuring outside his tent. He granted entrance, and the grinning faces of his commanders greeted him. Everything had gone according to plan – an amazing victory. He toured the camp, visiting the few wounded. Almost all of the wounded were on the Blue side.

His commanders begged and pleaded for two days that they should follow up on the victory and crush the remnants of the Blue army. But he could not allow it; he had killed all the Blues he could stomach. Near dusk of the second day, he informed his bodyguards that he was going for a walk alone to clear his head. They protested but he finally wore them down. No doubt they would still be close to him though hidden.

He walked until he came to a forest clearing, the perfect place to think things over. He paced, reviewing the ethics of what he had done. The Maroons needed him to be a Maroon master strategist commander so he gave that to them, ignoring that a short while ago and for most of his life he was a Blue scout.

He felt dizzy so he sat down on a tree stump. Suddenly he heard the sound of a long-range sniper shot.

He turned his face to the bullet.

The Final Fortress

Rebecca Laskowitz

There wasn't much time left. Philip knew this. The entire village knew as well. What did they have? Hours? Very unlikely. More like minutes. Minutes that flew by with increasing speed as the enemy drew closer. Philip looked at all they had accomplished. The walls were high and foreboding, but size was not enough to prevent annihilation. Strength was the key factor to guard against the great enemy, and Philip prayed to the gods that the fortress held strength.

The villages that had once stood here obviously lacked the strength needed to keep the enemy out. How many fortresses—great fortresses built with the blood and sweat of great men—had stood here before today only to be wiped away by one pass of the great enemy? There must have been hundreds, maybe even thousands, of towns that have been destroyed. Completely and utterly erased from the map.

There was no way for anyone to ever know the number of villages that had once stood here. The great enemy never left any traces of the civilizations it destroyed. There were no artifacts to be uncovered or histories to be remembered. It was as if they never existed and the great enemy was all there ever was.

But Philip knew better. He understood his village was not the first to face the great enemy, yet he prayed it would be the last. If he could defeat the great enemy, all other nations would bow down to him. They would come to him for protection, for wisdom, and for alliance. He would gain the respect of all the world's leaders. If he ever needed anything from anyone from anywhere, he would have no questions to answer. The thought was enough to make his chest puff up and his lips to form a triumphant grin.

Philip's smile disintegrated instantly, however, when a thundering crash jolted him back to reality. The enemy was approaching faster than he had anticipated and the odds of his victory were extremely low. His workers scrambled to finish the fortress to be used as protection from the oncoming attack.

Most of his people looked as terrified as he felt. He would never show his fear on the outside, however. He was, after all, their leader. Nothing could break the spirits of a civilization quicker than a leader admitting to fear and doubt.

Nonetheless, a fear was present in his heart that Philip could not squander. He looked at the structure being built for his village's protection and only saw towers that would crumple like paper, gates that would be knocked down with one swift blow, and walls that would surrender after one wave of attack.

The sound of the thunder grew louder letting all know the great enemy was advancing. Within a few minutes, the strength of the fortress would be tested. If it didn't survive the first wave, there was very little chance of it standing the second and third. The great enemy was very persistent and would not stop sending wave after wave of destruction until the village was no more.

As Philip focused on the sounds of onslaught, his gaze drifted to the sky. Several birds swarmed overhead, making circles around the highest towers. They showed no fear when they flew close to the fortress and then up to the sky again, as if taunting his workers. The birds were spies of the great enemy and hinted that the attack would begin any second.

Then, as if confirming his fear, one of the birds dropped a missile. A single missile fell from the sky in a direct path toward the highest tower. There was nothing Philip could do but watch. Upon being hit, the tower fell flat to the ground. It was as if a giant stepped on top of it in an angry rage.

"No!" yelled Philip, realizing his fortress would never stand against the great enemy.

"Philip!" came an even more powerful voice. Philip looked up into the eyes of a woman who seemed startled by his outburst.

"Sorry, mom," he said as he plopped down on the sand.

"I think you've had enough sun for today," his mother said. "And it looks like the tide is coming in."

Philip and his mother packed up their belongings and trudged up the beach. Philip risked one final glance back as the first wave of the great enemy washed over his fortress.

CHARACTERS

LIVE IN

STORIES

Writing through the words to your characters...

Now is the time to write. Empower yourself to deliver the stories that lie within. Break out the scrap paper, the simulated, onscreen paper, or the trusty, somewhat dusty notebook and write. Just sit down and do it. So far, we have focused on your muse...so, you should have the inspiration...and belief...without which your characters would not be real...wait a minute, they are characters...

Choose whether you need to outline your storyline or just jump into the writing. If you choose to outline, be consistent in formatting. Short or long outlines depend on the writer. With short outlines, you can save some of your words for the story itself and breathe life into the story. With longer outlines, you can simply fill in the empty spaces and provide transitions to your world of imagination. If you choose to just jump into the writing, feel the pen, pencil, or keyboard. Search deep inside for the inspiration and let your creativity flow through the writing instrument as you conduct your verbal symphony.

Think of topics with which you are comfortable. Remember though that being a writer involves writing. So, compose every day. Find a small space, find a time, find a reason to write. Enjoy becoming a part of your thoughts instead of the controller. Enjoy becoming a part of something bigger instead of just something. Enjoy being a writer.

The writings in this section delve into characterization. Watch the characters evolve and expand your own creations...

Each

Each night each moon,
Will come and close the afternoon,
And I will still be there in the shadows,
Awaiting my time to shine.

Each day, each sun,
Will close the night and darkness there is none,
Casting my shadow of the day,
What will I become.

I listen to my soul when all is still,
And it tells me I am real,
It tells me I am doing right,
Each sunny day, and moonlit night.

Skyler Wolf Jones

Alive

Cacy Ann Minter

I didn't know where I was when I woke up. I was aware of a pressing sensation on my chest, but couldn't figure out where it was coming from. I tried to look around and realized my field of vision was limited to the area directly in front of me. I couldn't move my arms or legs, or even swivel my head from side to side. I heard voices speaking frantically, but it was as if they were off at a long distance, as if they were at least a football field away. Other than the slight pressure on my upper body, I had no sensation or feeling whatsoever, other than a kind of heaviness I figured was just my brain coping with the paralysis I seemed to be experiencing.

I could see an open expanse of sky so I assumed I was lying prone outside of my car. I thought back as far as I could remember, but for the moment was just drawing a blank. Suddenly, the hazy form of a woman flashed into my view, moving just as quickly out of my range of sight as she had entered. Waiting patiently, I saw her hover in my line of vision once more, flashing a penlight into both of my eyes. At the time I didn't think about why that bright flash of light didn't blind me or cause me to blink, but I would later come to know why.

Searching through my vast knowledge of medicine, I tried to conjure up the specific types of disorders that might cause the condition I was experiencing at the moment. I immediately ruled out glaucoma and migraine as reasons for the peripheral vision loss. That left about ten or twelve other diseases and conditions as the cause due to the fact that I never before suffered from migraines and the stage of glaucoma at which such vision is lost is such an advanced stage, it would not have happened so immediately. I also ruled out the more rare eye diseases such as retinoschisis and retinal degeneration as those too would have taken too long a time to develop. Most of the other possibilities, such as Usher Syndrome or CAR Syndrome, would not quite explain the other symptoms that were occurring. Thinking back hard on my early medical training at the University of Texas, I decided I must have suffered a stroke. It would explain the heavy feeling in my body (although usually affecting mostly the side of the body, I was grasping at this point), the loss of vision, the loss of hearing, and possibly even the paralysis. Deciding I would rather settle on stroke than the dreaded 'brain tumor', I was helpless to do anything besides wait for aid at the hands of the woman whom I was now watching. She was shaking her head at something over her left shoulder. I knew that was not a good sign.

The woman moved again from my field of sight and I saw the sky before above me jerk a bit. Realizing I was probably being lifted onto a stretcher, I searched my brain for any memory that I could find of what events had recently transpired prior to my current semi-comatose state. I looked deeper and deeper into my mind and began to get a clearer picture of what probably had happened.

I had been on my way home from work at the clinic. I remembered waiting patiently for the stoplight at Anderson Mill Rd. to turn green and then proceeding through the intersection in my mind's eye. I recalled glancing to my left and seeing the headlights of a white Hummer racing towards me. As if in slow motion, I realized I would not make it through the intersection in time and braced myself for the imminent impact. The final memory I could bring forth was the feeling of my heading snapping to the right as I was struck on my driver's side door by the speeding vehicle.

My sky view soon was traded for the dull interior of an ambulance. I knew the dull throbs I could hear pulsating in the distance must be the warning siren of the rescue vehicle, but it sounded as if it was coming from another side of a long tunnel. I wondered how bad of shape I was in and when the paralysis would wear off, if ever. Hoping for the best, I saw rather than felt the ambulance grind to a halt as IV's and other medical equipment in the cab shifted and jerked spasmodically. I could tell I was being lifted again and rolled quickly down a long corridor. I silently prayed, although I had never done so before, to whatever God might be listening to guide the surgeon's hands as they put me back together.

My gurney was finally pushed into a dimly lit corridor after a short ride in what I was sure was an elevator. I wondered which local hospital I had been taken to, Seton Shoal Creek probably, as it was the closest. I had never been inside Seton before and didn't recognize the area now as I lay awake, wondering what was to become of me and whether I would be given intravenous anesthesia or a local one, depending on just what my injuries were. I knew that the most important thing the doctor's needed to do right now was deal with any internal injuries and blood loss. My temporary paralysis could wait.

I lay on the stretcher for what seemed like hours and had already grown quite confused by the time I finally saw an elderly gentleman lean over me. I thought that he had possibly already been operating on my distraught body the entire time I had been laying and thinking, I just hadn't been able to see him due to the loss of my side vision. However, I knew he should have had a small medical staff assisting him throughout the process and couldn't figure out why I had not seen any of them sliding in and out of my view. I wondered if I had even passed out and not realized it, but soon put that thought to rest as I realized I had been slowly counting, waiting for the sleep inducing drugs to work their magic. They strangely never did lull me to unconsciousness and I now began wondering if I might be comatose and dreaming everything that had been and was now transpiring. I again ruled this scenario out due to the fact that everything felt so real. Never in my wildest dreams could I have imagined any events as vividly as what I was witnessing now. Besides, if this had all been a dream, parts of it would have appeared jagged and disjointed as all dreams do.

I again saw myself being moved (I say saw because I could still feel nothing other than the 'heaviness' I have described to you earlier). Soon, all I was looking at was the briefest glimpse of steel mere inches away from my faces. Then all light left me and I stared into utter darkness.

I knew I was not unconscious because I could see minute flecks of dirt and other matter before me as my vision adjusted to the blackness that surrounded me completely. Panic began to set in. I knew after a few short moments of confusion that I the dimly lit room I had occupied only moments before was not an operating room, or even and ICU unit. It had no doubt been the Seton Shoal Creek morgue. I had been presumed dead and was now to spend my probably last remaining moments on this earth mistakenly locked inside a tiny refrigerated compartment until my wife claimed my body and funeral preparations began. I knew at that time it would be nearly impossible to tell when I had actually died as the cooling box I now occupied would delay decomposition for some time. I could possibly lay awake in the steel cubicle for hours or even days before I finally succumbed to the death sentence that had been passed on to me by incompetent EMT's. I vowed right then to find that woman who had given up on my limp body so carelessly and haunt her in my afterlife, whatever kind of afterlife was in store for me. As a self-proclaimed agnostic, I had never believed in much of anything other than the medicine I had so put my faith in for all forty-three years of my short life. I realized with horror that such faith had failed me at the most crucial moment. I was surely suffering from some form of inanimate suspension, such as the death-like coma caused by a toxin given off from the puffer fish. Since I knew I had not partaken of any exotic seafood dishes as of late, I could not figure out what exactly had happened, so I instead laid the entirety of the blame of my situation upon the clearly poor trained technicians who must have shown up at the scene of my car accident. I berated the fools over and over in my head for quite some time. I could not help but wonder how I could have been so careless as to be taken unawares by the Hummer in the first place. I wondered what fortune must I have had to be attended to by the world's two stupidest emergency personnel. What other poor souls had received this same malpractice at their hands? How many more would senselessly die? Would I be the first to somehow finally escape the grasp of death by the skin of my teeth and put an end to the suffering no doubt caused by the lazy offenders? Or would some other poor soul, completely unaware of my plight, suffer the same fate and miraculously awaken in their cold compartment and begin banging on the ceiling and walls of their confine, screaming for relief, begging for assistance and removal from the claustrophobic conditions? I could only wish the medical examiner who finds such a person would not be frightened into a heart attack, thus leaving the poor wretch to continue on to his or her untimely death with no help of rescue.

I lay in that steely box thinking such thoughts as these for what felt like hours. I had no way of telling how much time had passed. Although I heard my wristwatch ticking away unerringly somewhere far off, I was helpless to even simply raise my arm to look at it. Truly, even if my comatose condition had worn off and I had regained the use of my limbs, the tiny chamber in which I was now nestled would not have allowed for the slightest free movement of any sort. When my paralysis passed (and I hoped against all hope it would), I would have to scream and use my head and feet to pound on the interior walls of the cold box in what might be a vain attempt to arouse the notice of an attendant, if one was even still in the vicinity of the autopsy area.

For some unknown reason (although more than likely it was denial), I chose not to think about why I was still alive after spending so much time inside the refrigerated box. I knew there could not have been much oxygen in the miniscule room I was allotted. I at long length allowed my mind to rest on this matter, as if grasping onto a focal point instead of allowing my mind to wander might possibly salvage my sanity, which was already beginning to teeter on the brink of no return. I found myself making arguments about my state of existence, holding complete conversations with my inner voice (perhaps I had already passed the aforementioned brink, but best not to dwell on that).

"How could I possibly still be alive? How am I breathing? "

"The coma state you are in must have slowed down your heartbeat, thus making it possible to slow down your respiration to an infinitesimal amount, which has allowed you to live longer off of less oxygen intake simply because your body does not require a normal amount at this time. Consider it suspended animation."

"Suspended animation. Hmmmm, if I could market this to NASA somehow I could make millions!"

"You would have to get out of here first. What good is money to a dead man?"

"But what exactly caused this state for me? Was I injected with some sort of experimental drug by the EMT? Are they in fact using me, as they have possibly used others before me, to test this new drug out? Will they return to the morgue in the middle of the night to secretly remove my body and test the effects of this drug? Can I pray for relief at that time?"

"I wouldn't get my hopes up, buddy. Best to expect the worst and hope for the best in my opinion."

I assumed nothing at this point of my incarceration of both my body and my mind within my body. Even as far-fetched as the 'illegal drug experiment conspiracy' seemed, it was certainly better than facing the alternative silence I knew was awaiting me during every break in my interior discussions. I again commented (to myself of course) on the slight feeling of pressure that was the only sense I could feel. At some point in time I heard, off in the distance, a rapid squeaking noise, and momentarily shuddered inwardly at the thought of mice. Mice in a morgue box! And I had always thought Seton such a fine hospital!

I came to realize I could distinguish colors again and knew instantly that the squeaking I had just heard was not in fact rodents, but was the sound of the drawer door opening. I prayed that my moment of rescue had finally arrived. I wondered if the two criminals who had surely induced this state on my body had finally been found out and captured. Might they have shown some temporary remorse at their actions and enlightened officials to my condition? Was I now to be revived fully to a healthy state?

I saw readily that unfortunately this was not to be. I was again moved, that much I could tell. Back into the dimly lit room and again waiting in anticipation for whatever would come next. I looked and waited and watched directly above me as hard as I could. The lighting was soon amplified and I realized I was staring up into a set of fluorescent tubes. Every once in a while, the elderly man (who I correctly took for the ME) would come into focus for brief moments, only to sway out of sight again, then return some moments later. This went on for quite some time. I don't know how long it took me to realize what was happening. When I did, the last tiny fiber that had been holding my sanity intact finally snapped completely and irreparably.

He was performing an autopsy. On me.

I knew I had been in a car accident, but I hadn't been drinking, there was no reason for this! A thousand thoughts flew through my mind and no matter how hard I tried to silence them and pull myself together to work towards creating some sign of life for the morgue practitioner, I could not keep my brain focused on any one thought in particular. I began willing my finger to move, willing my chest to rise, even minutely, searching for any sign of surprise in the ME's eyes.

"I am not a cadaver!!!!! Look at me!!!!! Look at me breathing!!!! Look at my EYES!!!!!," I screamed silently. "Please, for God's sake, DON'T DO THIS!!!!! STOP AT ONCE!!!!!"

It was pointless. The man continued his grim work completely unaware of me. I remained conscious throughout the entire ordeal. I wondered how I could still be alive once he finally stood back and stripped the latex gloves off of his hands. I knew that if an autopsy had indeed been performed, my organs would have been removed. How could I now be possibly still alive?

And then I realized this: I was not. I had not been since the first time I had awoken from the accident. It was the only thing that made sense. It explained all of my symptoms. It explained why two well trained emergency technicians and a Morgue Examiner had not been able to sense the life flowing in me. There no longer was any life flowing in me. I was now locked with my thoughts, and my thoughts only, inside of a fleshy shell that would soon begin to deteriorate. I was locked with my own thoughts for perhaps all of eternity.

I somehow managed to make it through the entire embalming process without losing my mind completely and turning into a complete lunatic. I noticed with some pride that I was not singing songs to myself over and over again, or even ranting any longer. It was as if a sense of peace had come over my mind, not necessarily replacing the feeling of weight I had felt earlier, but instead I came to the realization that that was exactly what the pressure had been the entire time. It was my own mind battling against the calm that death had brought already to my body. My mind had refused this calm, up until the moment it was utterly impossible to deny the facts any longer. After finally accepting my fate, I began to steadily grow more and more serene.

The memorial service was quite lovely, or at least what I could make out of it seemed so. I recognized many faces leaning over my coffin and counted at least two hundred mourners in attendance. I never knew I had been so well regarded by so many of my colleagues and family.

As I now lay entombed in utter silence, I find myself thinking on why I never discussed with my wife the possibility of cremation prior to my passing. I lay in a vat of utter darkness save for the occasional worm or spider creeping over my line of vision. I know that my left eye has now been eaten away as my sight has faltered to a two-dimensional stare, and I am sure the right is soon to follow. I can't help but wonder if this is the Hell I have been condemned to suffer due to my lack of belief in God. I have had many years to wonder about this and have begun in the most recent times to accept that possibly I lived my life in error. I know now that I am at least not alone in my doom – some time back I heard distant thuds surrounding me and rested in the knowledge that my wife has finally joined me and more than likely now occupies the plot next door. I wonder whether my neighbors to the left, above, and below me are also sharing my fate. I have time now to ponder such thoughts and pray fervently to God that eternity comes with swiftness.

The Darkness of Past

Courtney Lyn Blystone

The streets of Kyoto were dark and not a single lamp nor house was lit. It seemed rather strange that there would be not a single soul in the town. Kat Myamouto was on her way home in the southern corner, when a solid black figure moved passed her. It created such a presence it nearly pushed her off her own two feet. Kat was startled feeling her red hair rise up and swish against her back. The figure crept its way up to what appeared to be a stone tower or maybe a castle. This tower had many windows, and like most of the town no light resonated from it. Her jade eyes gleamed with fear as she saw another young girl her age on top of the tower. It caused a sensation of chills to creep and crawl up her spine and down her arms. She had the feeling, either this was the wrong night to be lost in a familiar city or she was being watched. "Such a pretty girl.." The figure said. Its ice blue eyes gazed down at Kat. It had a plan for this newcomer.

Kat kept on walking down the street in nervous. Her heart pounding fast like she had just ran a mile in a jog or marathon. Her red hair became damp as sweat dripped down her face past her green eyes. She could taste the sweat as it moved down her cheek, following it down to her red lips. She was feeling more and more discomfort, walking, faster, faster still, and faster yet. The figure glares more, chuckling to herself lightly as she sharpened the knife within her hands. When all of a sudden, Kat had made it to the tower. 'This is not an illusion...' she thought, as the figure came down from the tower and transformed again, into a dog. It looked so innocent as it grabbed Kat's attention and lead her through the threshold into the tower. The dog-like persona lead Kat to a staircase where she sat with it. It looked at her

44

and began to speak, "Hello young girl." Kat looked at it like it was another illusion to lure her elsewhere rather on the path to the safe part of town. She shook her head, pretending she heard nothing, because this was becoming a weird nightmare. The dog spoke again, this time very stern, "Hello girl, you know you are one with your own sixth sense." Thunder began to rumble and echo throughout the tower as it did so outside. Kat's eyes widened at what she wanted to believe was a dog, but still refrained from saying nothing. There was a loud crash followed by a bright blue light. It had just now gotten worse, it had began to storm.

"Um, I guess I could be. Where has everyone gone in this town?" Kat stated as firm as she could without showing signs of nervousness.

It looked at her with its' ice blue eyes once more and smirked, "Darling, you're in another world...one where people like you are held in high regard...or killed." Kat's eyes grew larger than the rims of her silver glasses. She was not only now afraid of this new world, a scary figure, a talking dog, a thunderstorm, but of being KILLED.

"Not to worry my dear, we won't kill you...we are creatures not like others, we are shadow figures...and figures of shadows and of your own fears." the dog-like persona continued telling Kat. She wanted nothing more than to make her feel at ease but, this wouldn't work. She took his sentence like one of those IQ Test questions that she never got, and this made her quite puzzled.

"My fear is death...death and being alone." Kat stated to the figure as it transformed yet again, this time a woman. The womanly figure stood tall with blue eyes and long black hair. The black hair was just as long as Kat's. It stood up in its kimono-like robes and smiled at Kat, revealing its' next trick of transformation, Kat's fear since she was little-her mother. The fear rose in Kat's stomach, tying up in little knots. Each one, just as painful as the other, making her cringe inside.

((Background Information))

The maternal nature of Kat's mother isn't one for us to judge. Though this was what she looked as, the figure never could bring out the side Kat knew. The one that would call her out of her room just to shove her back in. Her mother was a foul woman, that never really expected much in her life or for Kat nonetheless. Her mother bore Kat out of wedlock and never really forgave the man that did this deed. He was an American businessman, that one day stopped into a brothel for a good time, and ended up bringing more than just a good time. Nine months later her mother gave birth to her and that was the first day of hell even before her mother ran. Kris Nakamura was her name, and all she was known for throughout Kyoto as a "slut." Before all that, Kat's mother was a beautiful, jaw-dropping woman. She had long black hair and blue eyes. She stood pretty tall for a woman and was always one to light up the room with excitement. One day, when she had enough of her husband's brutality, she left him. There were no longer money ties and when she became desperate she ran to Yosai Shikimori. He said she could work as long as she did not do anything to disgrace the Shikimori Clan of Southern Kyoto. Though this bruised her pride, she bore Kat, and ran to shelter in Northern Kyoto with the American businessman, also known as John Copenhagen. Within the next 5 years everything began to draw itself into darkness and Kris withdrew herself, only to die at hand to the Shikimori Clan of Southern Kyoto.

There is nothing but silence as Kat stared at the figure of her mother. She feared the worst would come of it and just started for the entrance, it had remained opened. The rain was thrashing about the streets like a bunch of cars caught in a rainstorm. Kat blinked once more as she glared and it seemed this whole darkness thing disappeared. It was no longer her in a room, surrounded by nothing but walls at what appeared to be a silhouette of her mother. She was back on the white sidewalk, walking down the busy street of Kyoto. The splashing noise began to create themselves once more as cars passed right on by. It had not only stormed in Dark Kyoto but now in reality. Rain was ever persistent in Kyoto, never once truly left the city. It may stop for days and days but then start up again. Just like the sun, which sets all year long in a different spot. However, on three days it sets in the same spot under Crux and rises back up. This too, was a cycle. Seems everything in life revolved in a circle. Kat walked down to her corner which she lived on and took towards her friend, Krinn. He was standing outside, looking as though he was waiting for her. Above his head he held a soggy newspaper, which he shielded his hair from the rain.

"Where have you been, I have been out here for hours ringing this doorbell?!" he exclaimed, relieved to see Kat, giving her a tight hug. She looked at him with a blank stare from her eyes. It was like the darkness had somehow succumb itself inside her.

"Nowhere important to you..." she replied, giving an awful look of deceit, eyes glowing red for a second.
This wasn't Kat at all, she usually was a perfectly normal teenage girl.

She was somewhat perky but never mean to Krinn. He was the only person that paid attention to that girl behind those distinguished glasses. He sighed at her response; however, he did wonder of that new sense he felt around her. It was no longer like she was a living, breathing, human being but a sinister person revolved around hatred. Kat smirked as she continued making her way passed Krinn to her penthouse. He was quite startled and just left it alone. 'There is no reason to worry.' he thought repetitively to himself. The darkness expelled itself from Kat's body. Once out, it slammed the door shut before Krinn entered. It locked the door and let out a laughter, not of one happy but one ominous maybe even demonic. Krinn frantically banged on the door as he heard the laughter and Kat's giggles, followed by the light in the room being absorbed. Again, it was all dark as Krinn pounded harder, he was heard but not acknowledged.

"KAT-KUN! OPEN THE DOOR! KAT...PLEASE!" he begged, continuing to pound about the door. He drew more attention than he wanted. The neighbors all walked out of their apartments and penthouses to the what seemed insane teenage boy. The maintenance man walked by and Krinn with all his might pulled him aside. "OPEN THIS DOOR! PLEASE..." he shouted at the man.

He got a look somewhat of his insanity but the man opened the door. When he did, he found Kat laying on the ground. The Darkness had created somewhat of an aura around her. It was floating above her like a cloud. However, Kat was giggling like a 5 year old at the playground. She was talking to it nonetheless, she looked 5 years old. Kat's head turned her attention to Krinn, "Wanna play?"

Krinn felt a cold chill blow from the window as he saw Kat rise up. She had in her hands a porcelain doll with curly blond hair with a blue bow and blue eyes. She giggled like a giddy child happily to the window. She leaned over the ledge still giggling and dropped the doll. It soar down from the floors above and smashed when it hit the cement sidewalk. Kat turned to Krinn with an evil tooth-filled grin. "Oops..."she said, smirking wider. Krinn had never seen Kat this way at all, this was not her normality at all. He wished he didn't feel the chill which kept him attentively staring at Kat. She went about her business like she did nothing and came back to the darkness. The darkness grew as it looked into the innocence of younger Kat, it seemed to feed off what energy grew around her. It seemed to make a loud suction sound when Kat screamed, falling to the ground, and out cold. The lights once again were restored, Kat was again 17 years old, and she seemed normal. She rose to her feet and saw Krinn gazing at her like some kid at the circus for the first time. She walked to him slowly as she adjusted her glasses. He slowly took one step back, then two, and out the door away from her.

"Krinn!" she called out, as he ran further down the hall.
Never once did she see fear in him, now she had. The darkness had scared the only man she loved away, what would be next? The darkness resumed its presence in the darkest corner of the penthouse, Kat's bedroom. It seemed to only take shape and take hold of Kat around nightfall. Otherwise, it seemed to just gather energy from passing energy influxes and other feelings around town. Krinn's fear only made it stronger as it could sense it making its presence through the window known.

Krinn ran down the sidewalk and down the street. His heart racing enough it seemed it was going to beat out of his chest. He wouldn't turn back and look, he just kept running. He was almost home, just a few more blocks. When finally, he reached the stoop of his parents house, he placed his hand on the stone banister. He was huffing and puffing, he hadn't stopped since he left Kat's which was just a little over a mile away. His mother walked outside to find him there, his face pale, his blueberry-colored eyes just blank, and the look of fear written all of him.

"Krinn-san?" his mother questioned.

She felt her way around to the final step to Krinn's face. His face was obviously soaked with rain and sweat.

"Come in now dear, you can't catch a cold...you have exams," his mother said, leading him to the front door.

Krinn walked fast up to his room and shut the door, locking it behind him. He turned all the lights and made sure the lights in the city below were still on. 'Thank God...' he said to himself as he rested upon his bed. His cold black hair lay on his pillow, which seemed to absorb all his sweat and soaked hair. 'What was that?' he thought with a loud sigh, he just laid beneath the fan. He watched the brown blades turn in their circular motion. It's chill was unlike that of the chill he felt when he saw young Kat throw her doll out the window. 'But why didn't I see it? If it fell..' he questioned his vision and what he saw. He sat there thinking more and more on it until his clock midnight, and he had a startling revelation-'Its an illusion!' he exclaimed to himself, and

decided to test his theory at school the next morning. He now thought
he could have a way to save Kat. From what? He didn't quite know yet,
but he would get to the bottom of it.

The next day, Krinn left his house to find Kat standing on the sidewalk.
He slowly made his way down the staircase, looking at her. He was still
a little freaked out by last night's strange happenings. This however,
didn't stop him from taking her in a secure embrace. She looked at
him, smiling lightly, and let go of him. She walked down the sidewalk
and began to mumble to herself. It seemed she might be plotting
something. They shortly arrived at the school and Kat stood there
staring. Krinn walked up to the door and opened it for her, as her body
walked up to the threshold of the door. That's when everything began
to slow down in perpetual motion. She entered with her eyes glazed
over, eyeballing her two least favorite students. They made eye contact
with her and all you heard were two thuds. Their bodies hit the floor as
Kat continued walking down the hall, Krinn stayed behind. He had his
hands on the metal centerpiece of the doorway, watching her. Kat
turned sharply into her Algebra class and went to the teacher, "Mr.
Hizumi...two students are passed out." she said, smirking evilly as she
turned away from him. Krinn walked into the room shortly after, and
drew everyone's attention to the hall. Mr. Hizumi was beside the two
unconscious students, frantically calling both their parents. Shortly
after that, investigators began to show up. They looked at the bodies,
searching for any physical evidence. While examining the female
student, Yumi, they found a baby blue ribbon with a light blond hair
strand. It looked as though it had came from the doll Kat had just
previously thrown out the window. Could it be possible the darkness
killed Yumi and also killed the male student, Miako? Kat felt an

overwhelming sense of guilt as they continued to investigate until they called in the paranormal investigators. They had no physical evidence so they had to use what they believed could be supernatural evidence. It was growing quite evident that the darkness was actually a form of Kat's anger, jealousy, or her hate. The reason Yumi was dead didn't seem quite that obvious, unless you bring out what happened years ago.

- – -FLASHBACK- – -

Kat and Yumi were at the playground playing in the sandbox when Miako came over. The three sat and built each of their own sandcastles, Miako's being well rounded with a fort around it, Yumi's the basic one with a draw bridge and mote, and Kat's however, seemed to be a looming tower. The friends were just having a great time, giggling amongst themselves, when a dog appeared out of no where. It didn't come close to the children, just watched them closely. As the dog sat there, it seemed to have red eyes that peeked from behind the bush where it was sitting. Maiko began to whisper to Yumi, "Knock over her castle..." Yumi was resistant at first it seemed because she'd argue back about how it was a bad idea and she didn't find it necessary to do that. Miako became angry and kicked over his castle, scattering sand everywhere, and getting it all over Yumi's pink dress and her eyes. The young girl became very angry as Kat sat entranced by this strange dog. "Fine!" Yumi exclaimed, kicking over Kat's castle with an abrupt force. It took Kat's attention away from the dog as it happened. She grew enraged and stood up, pushing over Yumi with such a force she fell backwards over the wood barrier of the sandbox. Yumi cried and yelped for help, she had busted her shoulder. Kat smirked evilly with a grin and looked at the girl. "Momma's here...I'll make you all better..." Kat said in an maniacal tone. Miako tried to interfere and get Yumi but Kat turned around and growled, "NO!" Maiko fell over too. He too, lie in pain, yelping for the teacher.

"Teacher...Teacher..."they cried and yelped. No one heard them, and soon there was silence, such a silence it was deafening. Kat picked up Yumi's doll and smashed it to the ground, shattered pieces of porcelain scatter the grass around the sand box. As recess ended, Kat walked away, leaving them to their suffering.

- — -

Kat looked at Miako and Yumi's bodies like the rest of the curious students that looked from the doorway. Her stomach in knots as one of the investigators turned to Kat giving her a strange look. "That girl, bring her here." the investigator said, pointing at Kat. The teacher allowed Kat out of the classroom and to the investigators. They examined her closely, invading her personal space. Her eyes seemed to go blank again, and soon the two investigators dropped like Yumi and Miako. A large number of gasps from the other students began and then ended as they saw Kat. Her aura around her became a dark black and everyone began to scatter. A young girl began to run towards Kat and entered her soul. Kat began to growl and throw a tantrum of a supernatural proportions. One student remained and looked at Kat strangely. The student tried to reach out and touch her, but once the hand hit Kat's porcelain skin, the student dropped dead. It seemed whatever had possessed Kat was killing off people or anyone that was trying to help her.

A dark cloud formed in the hall and rain drops began to fall. Following that, a young girl appeared again before Kat. Instead of being with her physical being, it stood beside her.

"Now, kill that one." it stated to Kat.

Kat smirked and soon the one person the young girl wanted dead, fell to the ground into a puddle. The rain that mysteriously began ended. It was now quiet and all of the students in the classroom eyeballed Kat strangely. She walked towards the class, only to have them shut the door and lock it. They now feared her and her little girl counter part. The young girl was still beside Kat, carrying with her a red rubber ball. She bounced it up and down, letting the sound echo around the whole entire school. It seemed everyone was squared away and totally frightened. Kat smirked and just walked out the door, the little girl followed. This little girl had jet black hair, violet eyes, and seemed very white in skin color. Whatever it wanted to do, Kat would do. Was this another minion of the darkness? Far from it, it was Kat's inner-child. Kat walked to her old Primary school and sat down on the swing. Her inner-child sat in the sandbox, playing with her ball. It was no longer bouncing, it was floating. Seems this child product of Kat was telekinetic. It played with the other children well until a young boy named Timmy tried to take her ball. "NO! MY BALL!!" the girl exclaimed, and Timmy fell out of the sandbox with a glare of the girl. The boy cried as he laid on the grass with many scratches from the wooden border. He cried loudly and when he tried to get up, the girl pushed him over again. "NEVER TOUCH MY BALL AGAIN!" the girl, said with such a force it scared Timmy more. Timmy left the box and ran all the way to the basketball court, sitting safely by the teacher. Kat looked at the child product and nodded at it. It just kind of gave her this look of the uttermost deceit. It smiled at her with a smirk and lightly moved towards her, sitting beside her. The girl held herself around Kat's arms like she was a daughter, not some child product. She lightly shifted her head side to side, allowing her blonde curls to bounce. Kat looked down at the girl noticing her baby blue ribbon was torn. It sent thousands flashbacks all at once to Kat's mind of what they found in Yumi's hand. The bell then rang for school to let out and before 20 minutes could pass, Krinn showed up. He saw Kat playing with the girl, doing one of those girl hand games.

"Candy apple on a stick..." they chanted, as Krinn sat amused. Krinn looked at the little girl, it reminded him of the doll Kat had in her room. She had always kept it on the top shelf and in high regard, like it was some kind of family emblem. The girl giggled and laughed as it sat there facing Kat. She smiled as Kat lost every time, until Krinn suddenly moved, and he had attracted himself to their attention, "Someone's here..." The young girl said, lightly pointing in Krinn's direction.

"That's Krinn, Sophie...he's my boyfriend." Kat replied with a giggle. He just stood there, trying not to make Kat angry by his presence. "Umm...hello Kat." he said with a shaky voice. He was more afraid to talk to her than the first night he saw her make friends with the darkness. Everything seemed normal because, Kat usually is one to laugh and have fun. The only thing strange was the young girl named "Sophie" that seemed to be around her now. The dog that Krinn had seen before it morphed into the darkness, could never be seen. It seemed it was either in a figure of a girl or a cloud of monstrous hate. The first time Kat saw it, it was in the shape of a girl with long black hair and blue eyes. Then after she gained its' trust enough not to kill her, it morphed into a dog. Dogs are considered man's best friend, but shortly after that it had became like the doll. This struck Krinn's curiosity, so instead of hanging around the playground, he went to Kat's apartment.

When he arrived, it seemed the place was as clean as before. He had to step over a few things here and there, when he eventually arrived to the attic door, he opened it. There were old tethered boxes and photo albums everywhere. Krinn decided to search through the albums, nothing but old photographs of Kat and her parents. He slammed the first one to the ground, creating a dust cloud. Sliding out came a picture of 4 people. It was Kat, her mother, father, and a little girl. The little girl looked like Sophie and the doll. This was quite unusual circumstances, but Krinn decided to flip the photograph over to see the names. It read off as follows: Kat-5, Mom, Dad, and little Sophie-2. Krinn's eyes widened as they focused on the last name in the list. It was like he was in utter confusion or shocked it was the little girl Kat was just saying was her best friend. This little girl wasn't Kat's inner-child, more so a ghost of some sort. There were papers in the little area where the picture had slid. It was an old newspaper clipping, it stated: "Young girl, Sophie Nakamura-Myamouto dies in drowning at Hakumi Bay." As he continued to read he was shocked by one detail: "Authorities are lead to believe the older sister, Kat Nakamura-Myamouto, aged 5, drowned the toddler..." Krinn's eyes widened more as he looked at that sentence repetitively.

The sentence just seemed to silence him. It's like it had this way of captivating whomever read it, drawing unwanted attention to it. Krinn stuck the paper clipping in his coat pocket and left the attic. Once he reached the bottom step, Kat stood right in front of him. She looked at him with an angry smirk.

"What were you doing up there Krinn?", she growled.

He stood silent in fear and stuck his hand into the coat pocket and pulled out the brown paper. He looked at Kat, "You did this, you killed your sister." Kat gulped lightly, you can see her swallow the spit as it went down. He eyeballed her as she stood there silent but smiling. She nodded up and down with the smirk still stuck to her face. Sophie came up behind Kat and grabbed her hand. "Now it's your turn..." Kat said as evil as she could. She pushed Krinn's body to the ground and proceeded to get on top of him. Sophie handed Kat a silver dagger from inside her white stocking. Kat looked at him dead in his eyes and chuckled, stabbing him violently. Over and over again the dagger entered and exited the body. Blood began to accumulate on the dagger, causing a great puddle beneath Krinn. She laughed out loud, spreading the blood which was on her hands, all over the wall. Leaving behind handprints as she dug it into him, his eyes began to get lifeless. She snickered evilly and got up off him, lightly placing the knife beside her. She watched the blood form on the floor and leaned down near Krinn's ear, whispering, "Krinn...you can wake up now." Krinn's last words were uttered, "Wake...up....?"

"KRINN! WAKE UP! TIME FOR SCHOOL!" his mother called, as

Krinn rose up out of bed. He was breathless and covered in a cold sweat.

"It was just a dream, only a dream.." he said, catching his breath as he looked at the clock, its green numbers saying,"8:15a.m."

GROW

YOUR

STORIES

Engage a New Outlook...

As you enter each new year, you realize it can be full of fun, full of frenzy, full of excuses not to write that new story, poem, novel, play, or check...There are always resolutions around writing if you are a writer. There are also at least double the excuses for every resolution going unfulfilled. The only one who can build your story is you. Your neighbor, your writing group or buddy, your small pet can only encourage the story to start, stop, or spin. You must engage in the actual writing. The inspiration was not meant for anyone else. Choose to write the story that connects to you.

You know what your day looks like. You know when you have time to write. You also know when you don't have time to write. There are really two challenges though...Finding the time when you are not asleep and finding your particular muse somewhere along the way. They are both elusive creatures. Neither seem to be on your side. Neither want to cooperate with each other. You may be inspired, but you don't have the time. You may have the time, but are not inspired.

The writings in this section took time to assemble, research, and connect. As you look to engage a new outlook, consider the time you need to grow your stories...

Babbling For...

A mind is a terrible thing to...
Waste not want...
Not on your...
Life is not...
Easy come, easy...
Go to the front of the...
Line-jumping is not...
Permitted to run...
Wild-goose...
Chase your...
Dreams can come...
True love comes from the heart, not the...
Mind over...
Matter of life and...
Death warmed...
Over my dead...
Body, mind, and...
Soul means of...
Inspiration.

John E. Murray, III

Too Low For Dinner

Bryan Kaminsky

Dark clouds spanned the early afternoon sky as Edward walked out of the back door of the storage room of a florist. Edward was wearing a black cloak, ripped black jeans, and a black shirt. Edward liked the color black because it absorbed every spectrum of light, and he liked to absorb any information he could obtain or observe.

He was carrying a rare plant which most people do not think of owning, growing, or planting. It was a carnivorous plant. Its appearance is similar to the ones people think of being located in jungles. It had a stem, a big mouth with teeth which could snap, and thorns. It was small though, smaller than the pictures seen of them in a jungle habitat.

Edward approached his car, a black sedan with lightly tinted windows. He owned a black car for the same reason he wore black clothes. He got behind the wheel and placed the plant on the floor in front of the passenger seat. Edward thought to himself as he did each step, "put key in ignition, start engine, move stick, pull out, and drive." He drove seven miles to his apartment in a neighboring town.

Upon arrival he parked the car, got out, hid the plant under his cloak, and walked to his room. Along the way someone asked what he was hiding under that cloak of his. He grunted and responded, "An artist does not reveal his work."

After getting to his apartment he walked to his back room which he referred to as his "working studio" and put the plant down on the floor in a corner to the left of a window. The rest of the room was completely empty except for one wall. Against this wall was a mahogany desk with a computer and art supplies on it. Next to the desk was a tripod with a camera on top, and next the tripod was various lamps and lights.

Edward opened a drawer in the desk and pulled out a few lenses and placed them on top of it. He walked over to the lamps and lights and grabbed two; one in each hand and placed them on the long window sill under the window he put the plant next to. He plugged them in and turned them on.

Edward went to his desk and turned on his computer. He opened up his uploaded photos to get inspired. Photos of people, dogs, cats, trees, benches, flowers, and buildings flashed on the screen. He scrolled past one after another until he stopped at one of the side of an old church with mice eating garbage. His eyes lit up at the sight of this. He had been reunited with inspiration again. He left the room, and did not come back until two hours later carrying a cage of mice, wood, nails, and a hammer. He put the cage down on the right side of the desk and the rest in the middle of the room. Edward sat down on the floor and started nailing pieces of wood together to make a right angle one foot high and four feet in each direction. He went to another drawer in his desk and pulled out a paint brush and wood stain. His floor was made of wood and he liked to use the same stain on any wood he brought into the room for his art. He stained the wood, and pushed the right angle into the corner of the room the plant was in. Edward then opened the window to air out the room of the retched smell of wood stain.

Edward turned off the lights and left the room walking to his bedroom in his two bedroom apartment. This bedroom was actually used as a bedroom and had an actual bed in it. The room was usually kept too dark to distinguish what else is actually in it besides the king sized mahogany bed. He took off his cloak and jeans and lay down in the bed to go to sleep. Edward closed his eyes and did not open them again until it was 9:33 the next morning.

The room was still really dark because he kept black clothed blinds down at all times to keep the room dark. He put his jeans and cloak back on and exited his room to go back to his "working studio." Edward entered the "working studio" and yawned. He checked the stained wood to see if it was dry; it was. He went back across the room and got the cage of mice. He released the eleven mice in the cage to run around in the corner around the carnivorous plant.

Edward went to his desk and grabbed his camera. He started snapping pictures of the mice running around the plant until he finished the roll of film. Edward walked back to his bedroom with his camera, and shut the door. He hit a switch, but a regular light did not turn on.

Apparently his bedroom was also a photo development room. Tables lined one of wall of the room with bins on them. Along another wall was clothesline with photos hanging down from it developed. Edward took the roll of film out of his camera and began to develop his film. He lay down on his bed to take a nap. A few hours later he woke up and looked at how the photos looked. An expression of dissatisfaction appeared on his face, and he walked out of the bedroom. He did not like the pictures he took.

He put a new roll of film in his camera and left the room again to go back to the "working studio" and was pleased to see that nothing died in the corner. He turned on his two lamps, and grabbed two more, and then another two. He scattered them around the room, plugged them all in, and turned them on.

A shadow appeared behind the carnivorous plant. Edward's eyes lit up again, just like how they did when he saw the picture of the old church. He realized that he will use shadows to his advantage.

He began moving the lamps and lights around until he got shadows on the mice as well. He started snapping pictures. He stopped and moved the lights around a little more and got more shadow mice on the floor. He began snapping pictures again until his roll was finished.

Edward walked over to his desk and placed the camera down on it. He raised his arms in the air, looked at the ceiling, and shouted, "On this roll of film is the moneymaker!"

He turned toward the corner and pointed in its direction, and said "Tomorrow you all go back to the stores you came from."

Edward, lay down on the floor, and starred at the ceiling. He whispered to himself, "I will call it 'Too Low for Dinner'." He stood up, turned off the lights, and grabbed his camera.

Edward exited the room closing the door behind him leaving the room dark. He had done it. He had taken the picture that was going to get him enough money to keep his apartment.

Honesty Is

Aaron Eugene Lee

Frosted Flakes, or Wheaties. Cheerios are all gone: only two little o's remain. The boxes are full of words like "Best" and "Brightest". "Be all you can be", that's our army's slogan. Tiger Woods ate the Wheaties, I wanna be like him. The tiger says his are "Grrrrrrreat!" I gotta be the best, brightest and fastest. And I wanna have my breakfast with some toast. The toaster is on the other side of the table. A real problem. I groan, and then come to my senses. I grab the small card table and wrench it sideways, knocking some silverware and the salt shaker on the floor. I made a mess, but I get the toaster.

Since my wife can't help me, I help myself to the bread cooking machine. It takes too long to heat up so I pop it early and just stuff my face with cold rye. It is cold and it is rye. It is also dry. My mouth is full of this dry rye bread – I chew it loudly and my wife just scoffs.

I think she lied to me last night. I think she lied for me last night. Last night in bed I dreamed of rye bread. This morning has fulfilled my wild dreams of the night before. Have you ever woken up from a dream just to have the dream fulfilled?
I had to.

I had to buy my wife's lie. Eat it up like I was eating the toast. We don't always talk when we go to bed together. Sometimes we just lay there and dream before we nod off to dream. It seems that we wish for things. Me and my toast. Her and her lie. That's all it was, a little white lie. What does a white lie mean in the midst of life. Ask me, or ask my wife. My wife will tell you it means a great deal. That Honesty is important. That Honesty is secure, safe, binding, and sure. Honesty is all of these things. Ask me and I will say that a white lie in life is like a piece of cold rye toast and an opened salt shaker on the floor.

I beat my wife to the floor that day. She was going to clean up the spill, but I insisted. I got there before her. She had a rag – but I had my napkin. How unexpected was I that morning? You see, I rarely get a napkin to eat my Wheaties, or my Frosted Flakes. But that morning was different. She was about to clean the mess – but I beat her to it. I got there first. I made the mess, and I would clean the mess. I didn't really need her there. Not for that. What is a white lie in the midst of life? It is only a small mess that I can clean up myself...that, and a cold piece of toast.

After dropping the salt, I thought it was like losing a part of myself. We are all made of salt. 'From ashes to ashes and dust to dust'. What about 'from salt and to salt we shall return'? I thought maybe we were all just a little white lie in the midst of some one else's life. I have now given up my salt, and lost my dust.

Before I go to work in the morning I have a kind of ritual. I suppose we all do. I do. My wife does, and I do. I remember my parents having their own morning ritual, so I suppose we all do. I step in the shower, and then back out. I forget my toothbrush. I keep my toothbrush in the cabinet – but I brush my teeth in the shower. So I need to remember to take my toothbrush in the shower. Kills two birds with one stone, I say. My wife won't shower with me because I brush my teeth. I thought she was strange when we married, but the longer you live with someone the more you learn to love them. Her ritual begins with cleaning up after me (except for that one morning) and then avoids me in the bathroom. She won't even come into the adjacent bedroom if I'm still getting ready. She complains about the steam and my singing. Of course she compliments my singing on occasion. I think it just depends on what song I sing that morning. This talk is tiresome – no one wants to hear about how I brush my teeth after cleaning up after myself.

My morning ritual progresses, as does my wife's (and everyone else's I suppose). I head off to work and the rest of the day is rather uneventful. Not to suggest that nothing exciting ever happens, but just to say that I've gone on about my day too much already. I want to talk about THAT day. Just THAT day. When I ate Wheaties and Frosted Flakes because the Cheerios were all gone except for two. If you can understand that day then you may believe me when I say I have seen the CHILD of MERCY and MERIT. It was a circumstance that day. Something happened that changed my world. That changed my wife's world. It was OUR world really, and what changed was between us. We were visited that day, though we never fully introduced ourselves. Our visitor came and left, like visitors tend to do, but ours left us with a gift. Whoever came and went left us feeling silly. Stars silly. That is, so silly that we felt we were seeing stars. I dropped the salt and lost my dust. She came to help and I helped myself. At first it seemed like an act of rejection, and hers of retaliation. But when all was said and done I looked at her fine curves. How she filled out that dress very nicely. How she moved with grace and her shadow had trouble keeping up appearances with the real deal. My wife. So lovely, even if she did what she did. How could she stand it at all? Why hadn't she left me yet? Not that we ever fought – not really. Not that there were ever harsh words between us. Or threats, or fists, or fires of passion. I had swallowed my toast, but I wanted a second helping now. Honesty is brutal.

My wife, the queen of bees. She could have had her pick right out of high school, but she held out for me. We didn't meet until we were both out of college. What does that mean? I mean – I wasn't likely to meet anyone, and her...she could have had them all. But we met each other and now we were here together. The queen of bees and the jack of trades. But what could I do for her? The answer that came to me was my brain child. An idea so inspired that I think it was also left for me by our visitor. Something just for me. Just for me to give to her. I brushed my teeth before getting in the shower that morning. She knew about it too, because she passed through the bedroom that morning. Maybe that was her gift to me. Another chance. She saw me and I her. We both knew that my morning ritual had been set aside. And after that we made love and I called in sick to work. We wanted to spend all day together, but after our passionate throws we knew it was kind of like the salt and toast. Except maybe it was a little better that morning, after the sex. Though we didn't spend all day together it felt like we did. She said she had urgent business in the office and couldn't just call in sick. This was the real world and the real world needed her. I told her I understood – and that morning I think I did.

What did I do all day? It was like lying on a bed of nails. Not necessarily fatal, but if you try and get comfortable it makes things worse. She came home, and we saw each other again. We could still tell. That morning hadn't been a dream. There was still something between us. Given to us by our visitor. Maybe the world didn't change because of it – but something did, something just between us. Honesty is indirect. My wife may have lied to me the evening before, and she may do it again. But not every night, and I love her for it.

The only other spectacular thing about that day was my dream. Not the dream I had while I slept, but I'll tell you I met my wife that night. It was before that, when we laid down together and just breathed beside each other. We dreamed before we fell asleep. I couldn't tell what she was dreaming, but I'll tell you mine. I dreamed of the Honesty between us. What did it mean to me? Honesty is a one way ticket to the deepest part of a person's soul. It is a dark ride, and I have found myself frightened by it. But I ride the train and stare out the black window until the daylight comes back. Dark windows also provide a good reflection, but I did not turn away. I looked into the window anyway, seeing myself in the dark. The shadows beyond took shape and I saw a bird. A Crane. A beautiful bird that swooped down to the ground. It was flying. No, it was falling and it was lying. The bird of lies was headed for the ground and there might not have been enough air to slow it's descent. I wanted to scream out. To tell it to stop, to break its own fall. But that is not Honesty. So I prayed. Move into the fast lane, Crane. Die quickly, Dye your feathers red. Do not stop, do not hesitate, do not think that you can save yourself but give in. If death awaits you, be Honest.

My dream got me sweating a little bit, and my hand started to shake. My wife grabbed hold of my hand and I was able to stop, and sleep throughout the night.

Home Sweet Home
Rebecca Laskowitz

Sparky lay under the tall oak trees that dot the backyard. Furry animals scamper up the tall trunks and duck in crevices that they delightfully turned into their humble abodes. Every few minutes she can hear acorns hit the ground around her like tiny meteors. One occasionally finds its way to Sparky's head or paw to which she responds with a mere twitch and a grunt.

Sparky savors these moments under the trees. The stray acorn is gladly received over objects that come down on her tiny body in the house. It's a wonder that her twelve-inch frame is still intact after the way she has been treated all these years.

My owners don't like me. They never have. Why do they even have me?

It is said that Cavalier King Charles Spaniels are able to adapt to any environment.

Whoever made that up is clearly a human.

Sparky's treatment in the house can best be compared to that of a doormat, only not as glamorous. She spends most of her time locked in a cage in the laundry room next to the dryer and a box of wire hangers. Her coat that used to be silky and lustrous has lost its natural beauty.

This isn't where I'm supposed to be. I'm supposed to be with people, with children, with other dogs—not in a cage next to a hot vibrating machine that causes my hair to poof up.

The machine never stops. As long as the clothes keep coming, the machine keeps going. The smells of detergent and lint have inundated her coat causing her to always smell like socks and t-shirts.

Light from the sun peeks through the trees and causes small bright spots to dance on Sparky's paws. A small rumble comes from Sparky's tummy at regular intervals throughout the day. Meals are not something that Sparky has come to expect frequently. Her large eyes squint as hunger pangs fill her seven pounds of bone and flesh. Her meager frame makes anyone who looks at her only see a dingy coat and brown eyes that are set slightly too far apart. Her chestnut ears lay limp over her eyes as if they too have given up any hope of being cared for.

Sparky is let outside twice a day by the maid. It isn't often that her owners let her out, or do anything to care for her at all, for that matter. Their lives are full of more important events and caring for a dog is a waste of time. Coming up with a proper name for her wasn't even on their to-do list. Sparky was chosen for its simplicity and lack of originality.

They had to give me a boy name, didn't they? They probably don't even know that I'm a girl. Not that that's important or anything.
Sparky doesn't quite notice the hunger pangs anymore when thoughts of what her life has become start pouring rapidly into her mind. Who

needs food when no energy will ever be exerted? She is either in the laundry room or under the oak trees. Trying to cross over to the sunnier side of the yard produces an electric shock that lifts her off the ground. A wooden fence separates her from the quiet street where other dogs march happily alongside their masters.

Sparky begins to doze off when noises from across and down the street reach her ears. She fixes her eyes on the corner house from which emerged a tall white boxer with a football stuck between his teeth. Sparky inches her way to the edge of the fence closest to the house to get a better view of this white monster. Rapid movement in his stubby tail indicates massive enjoyment of his current activity. Today it's football. Yesterday was puddle hopping. The day before that was chasing rabbits. Everyday brings a new adventure to his paws. That's a fine place for a dog.

"Inside!" shouts the maid in her shrill voice.

Till next time, thinks Sparky as she tore herself reluctantly from the one glimpse of happiness she knew.

* * *

Sparky lies in her cage next to the silent dryer. It is the middle of the night, the only time when the dryer remains dormant for an extended period of time. The house is anything but silent, however, as a massive thunderstorm roars outside the naked window. The tops of trees can be seen from her cage swaying in the gusty wind like dark giants with many arms reaching for something to grab onto. The laundry room glows for a split second followed by a loud cracking sound. Sparky shakes in fear and lowers her head onto the newspaper that serves as her bedding.

There are a few moments of silence after the storm's grand finale. The silence is broken, however, by the chime of the grandfather clock. Three o'clock. She'll be let out in four hours and fifteen minutes for twenty minutes. She begins to close her eyes when a thunderous crash is heard outside. Sparky jumps up onto her paws, her eyes staring unblinking out the dark window. After what seems like hours, Sparky spins around five times before lying down for the rest of the night.

* * *

A giant hand lifts Sparky up by her scruff before she can open her eyes. She is carried to the back door and dropped onto the damp porch. The maid retreats back into the house without looking back.

Sparky staggers down the steps, still drunk with sleep. Her eyes look up at the trees and squint at the sun shining through the branches.

The grass doesn't grow anymore in the small corner of the backyard closest to the street. Instead of tulips and daisies thriving in the warm sunlight, droppings decorate the dried out lawn. Mounds of dirt can be seen next to deep divots that result out of boredom. There are never any toys to play with, and certainly never any humans with open arms to run towards.

Under the oak trees is a blanket of acorns that were used as missiles for target practice. The only form of contact the poor dog ever makes with other furry creatures are snickers and tail flips from the squirrels running free in the branches above.

If one were to go digging under the soft dirt at the base of the tallest tree—and no one ever went digging under the tallest tree—a buried treasure would be discovered. A yellow sock, the color of gold, along with a red sock, a green sock, a blue and white striped sock, a brown trouser sock, a gray sweat sock, white ankle socks—socks of every color and size are forever kept hidden in the hole under the blanket of acorns under the tallest tree. Sparky's treasure.

For months, single socks have left the laundry room without their partners. Sparky would smile to herself whenever someone walked into the laundry room looking confused with only one foot dressed. Her revenge was small, but it was still something.

Sparky's paws sink into the soft ground. She sniffs around for a few seconds before choosing a spot to do her business. She sniffs around some more. The smell of wet grass fills her nose and makes her sad. The smell of nature, of open air, makes her think of the freedom she will never have. She walks alongside the fence slowly, stopping every once in a while to observe an ant toiling over muddy mountains.

Her journey along the fence stops abruptly when Sparky comes upon a strange sight. Part of the fence has been turned into smaller sticks and splinters. A large branch from the tree above lies in the middle of the wreckage.

Sparky stares dumbfounded at the mess for a few seconds. She has never seen anything like this before in her life. She can clearly see for the first time the street which is usually blocked by the fence. Instead of gaps between wooden posts, she can see the entire picture at once.

Sparky can see birds across the street drifting about in the wind and landing in their makeshift homes high in the sky. Rabbits and chipmunks run amongst the well-groomed lawns of the houses lining the block.

Sparky turns around and looks back at her own house. With the exception of the broken fence, it looks pretty much like every other house on the street. Sparky knows better though as she trudges back towards the porch steps. She wonders why the maid let her out without having the fence fixed first.

Maybe she doesn't know the fence is broken. Well, if they ever want to show me how much they don't like me, just leave a big hole for someone to come and dognap me. Or let me go for a walk by myself and get lost forever.

Sparky stops dead in her tracks, terrified by that last thought. Go for a walk and get lost forever. It isn't the unknown world that sends the chills down her spine. It isn't the idea of being a seven pound foot long cavalier with half her teeth already missing in a dangerous world she has never explored before that makes the hair on her back stand tall. No, that doesn't scare her one bit.

It's the fact that she would welcome all those dangers with her tail happily wagging that terrifies her. It's knowing that if she's caught, she will be brought back her and away from freedom forever. Her owners would probably never let her outside again without a leash.

It is then that Sparky's thoughts are interrupted by the sounds of squirrels scampering up the tall oak tree. They get up to the branches, play tag and have the times of their lives. Sparky turns back toward the street with her mind made up. She carefully walks over the wooden rubble and stops when she gets to the curb.

This is a bad idea, she says to herself. Sparky takes two steps onto the street when a loud honk sends her wheeling around and scampering back to the sidewalk. She feels a strong gust of wind when the red sports car flies by. A terrible idea. Sparky turns back towards the other side of the fence.

* * *

"Dennis! No!"

Without looking back, Dennis rounds the corner of the hallway, his nails clicking against the slippery wooden floor. A pink fluffy slipper which he has taken hostage dangles in his slobbery mouth. He loses his balance when he turns another corner and bangs his head against the white painted wall. He does not seem to lose focus as his grip on the slipper tightens and he continues his great escape.

"What's he doing now?" calls the father from the refrigerator.

"He stole my slipper again!" shouts the daughter.

Dennis scampers into the den and attempts to hide the slipper under the couch when the father appears in front of him with a piece of cold pizza in his hand. "Leave it!" he shouts with such ferocity that the ceiling fan shakes. Dennis skids to a stop, drops his victim, and takes off in the other direction nearly mowing down the daughter as she runs into the room.

"Why does he listen to you?" she asks.

"Because," the father replies with a smirk, "I'm a man." He turns back towards the kitchen and the daughter retrieves her sopping wet slipper. Dennis does a few laps around the house, occasionally knocking into a wall or a doorframe. The bottom halves of all the doors and walls in the house have dents and scratches from years of Dennis's wild antics. The doors to the bedrooms and bathrooms must be kept closed at all times. Dennis manages to wreak some form of havoc in every room he gets himself into. After months of obedience school, he is the only dog to have failed in his class.

Dennis decides he does not want to stay cooped up in the house anymore. He heads for the backdoor in the kitchen and goes outside through the doggy door.

"What a beautiful day!" he says to himself as the smell of autumn fills his wet nose. He runs around the perimeter of the backyard making sure not to get jolted by the electric fence. Dennis does not really understand why his owners put up an electric fence. He would never run away. Everything that could possibly make him happy is in this backyard.

Dennis pounces on his big red football causing it to squeak beneath his paws. He takes it in his mouth and runs as fast as he can from one end of the yard to the other. He comes to a halt when he hears the garage door open and the car engine start. He looks at the red sports car as it passes with the father and daughter waving at him. He becomes sad when they leave because he always has so much fun with them. Every minute they are gone feels like an hour to Dennis.

He watches them speed away, and his heart skips a beat when he sees something hop into the road directly in front of the car. He leaps forward but an electric pulse sends him retreating back into his yard. It takes a few seconds before he regains his composure and looks to see if whatever leapt in front of the car is still in one piece.

It was probably a squirrel. They never have any sense when it comes to crossing the street.

Having thought this, Dennis is shocked to see a tiny dog hobbling across the sidewalk away from the street. His curiosity piques when he notices a branch that crushed the fence leading to her yard.

"Hey!" he calls out. The tiny dog stops between the sidewalk and the ruined fence. She slowly turns but can't find where the voice came from. "Over here!" She looks at Dennis with her large eyes and inches her way back to the curb. "You better look before you cross this time!" She looks and doesn't see any traffic. Her pace is slow as her nerves increase. "Hurry up! I won't bite you or nothin'!"

The tiny puppy—Dennis figured her to be less than a year old based on her size—finally manages to cross to his side. He hops up and down in excitement at the thought of a new furry playmate. His excitement subsides, however, when he sees the fear in the eyes of the approaching stranger. A peculiar sensation overcomes him, one he is quite unfamiliar with. Something inside him starts to feel bad. The little dog finally approaches him and sits down, not knowing what else to do.

"Hi," says Dennis, his voice a little shaky. The other dog just licks her lips. "I'm Dennis."

Dennis has to strain his ears to hear her barely audible response. "Sparky."

"Sparky?"

"Yes."

"Why are you whispering, Sparky?"

Sparky looks around, paranoid that she will be discovered. "Well, I'm not exactly supposed to be here."

"Your owners will understand," Dennis replies. "You just want to play, don't you?"

"I guess so," says Sparky, still looking around. A scream is heard from across the street in Sparky's yard followed by the maid seen running frantically by the shattered fence. Without thinking, Sparky darts past Dennis and under the porch steps leading into his house. Dennis spins around in confusion and follows Sparky under the steps.

"Okay," he says. "I'm officially confused. What just happened?"

"Don't make me go back there! Please, don't make me!" It is dark under the porch, but Dennis can hear the tears in Sparky's voice.

"Why? Why don't you wanna go back?" Dennis waits for her response but all that he hears is a low rumbling sound. "Are you okay?" Sparky whimpers and Dennis understands this will be the extent of Sparky's answer. "Hold on a sec." Dennis goes out from under the porch and looks back across the street. The shouts from Sparky's yard have died down and Dennis cannot see anyone else outside. He runs back to the porch and ducks his head down to look underneath. "Hey. Hey, Sparky. Follow me."

Dennis's heart aches a little when he watches Sparky slowly rise to her feet. Every one of her movements seems like it saps all her energy. He leads her up the steps and into the kitchen through the doggy door. "Here, you can have this," he says to her indicating his food bowl on the floor.

Sparky's eyes light up. "Really?" She doesn't wait for Dennis's response. Her face buries itself in the bowl, and for the next five minutes, the only sounds heard are Sparky's contented grunts.
"You know you should really slow down. Food won't do you any good if it comes right back up again."

Sparky pauses from her meal and looks into Dennis's eyes. "Thank you so much." Dennis smiles and Sparky turns back to the food.

* * *

"So can you tell me the deal with you and your owners?" asks Dennis. Sparky and Dennis lay in the grass in his backyard, the bright sun making it unusually warm for November. Colorful leaves surround the dogs attracting even more warmth and making them feel cozy.

"They don't like me," Sparky answers.

"And," Dennis coaxes.

"And what? They don't pay any attention to me except to hit me or toss me into a corner. My owner's son actually takes pleasure in throwing me across the room into the couch."

"That's terrible," says Dennis.

"Yeah, and it gets worse when he drops me on the floor when he's done, and then

I get in trouble for walking on the carpet."

"I can see why you don't want to go back," replies Dennis. Before the conversation can continue, the sound of the garage door is heard. Sparky goes to hide under the porch while Dennis runs inside to greet his owners.

Sparky settles under the porch and uses these moments of silence to contemplate all she had been through that day. The maid woke her up and threw her outside; she walked around the yard and discovered a doorway to freedom; she was almost run over by a car; she finally learned the name of the frisky white boxer across the street; she ate a whole meal undisturbed; she made a friend...A friend. A brand new and very welcome concept to Sparky. Things almost seem too good to be true. In the midst of remembering all the good things of the day, one more thought circles back through her mind: What's next?

* * *

The rest of the day passes without any real excitement. Dennis tells Sparky to stay under the porch when his owners are home. She watches him run around the backyard chasing the tennis ball the father throws. She is amazed at how well Dennis's owners treat him and how much they seem to truly love him.

* * *

The wind rushes through her hair with the intensity of ten tornadoes. She spins around at such high speeds that it is impossible to count the revolutions before beginning her descent back down to earth. The sides of her lips are involuntarily pushed up towards her ears giving anyone who catches a glimpse of her the false impression of joy and happiness. Her ears look just as happy as they dance in the wind, standing tall on the way down.

Her tummy is facing some direction that would confuse a compass when her soaring journey comes to an abrupt stop. She feels a soft pillow against her left cheek and her right ear flops down over her eyes, blocking her view. This is probably for the best since the only view available is of swirly blobs and red and white spinning in a black hole leading to another world—probably a better world.

She barely has time to catch her breath before the giant hand lifts her up by her scruff. She tries to prepare herself for her next soaring journey set to commence in five seconds. "Five! Four! Three! Two!" GONG! GONG! The sudden chime of the eighty-year-old grandfather clock loosens the hand's tight grip and sends her on a more direct path to earth. Her body is no longer greeted by pillows and cushions, rather by an expensive Oriental rug that she is never allowed to walk on.

The owner of the giant hand finds the remote control on the coffee table, finally losing interest in her misery, at least for the moment. She manages to make her way onto her tiny paws and out of the living room tripping several times over her tail. The world continues to do somersaults around her. The Power Rangers theme serves as her glorious exit music.

* * *

Sparky wakes up from her nightmare even more convinced that she cannot return to her house. She stretches her paws in front of her and peers out from her hiding place. Seeing the coast is clear, she runs into the backyard to do her business as well as do a little exploring.
The flowers smell so much nicer over here.

"Sparky!" Sparky turns towards the voice and sees Dennis running down the porch steps.

"Geez, you scared me."

"Sorry," Dennis says, "but you really shouldn't be walking around. Someone might see you."

"I know," replies Sparky. "I just needed to run around for a while."

"I know what you mean," says Dennis. "When I first came here, my owners used to keep me locked up whenever they left the house. I think they were afraid of me destroying the house or something." Sparky laughs, appreciative of finally having a normal conversation with another dog. "Oh," says Dennis, "don't move." Dennis runs into the house and returns quickly with a meaty bone. He drops it in front of her. "I thought you might be hungry."

Sparky finds herself overcome with emotion. She leaps towards Dennis with energy she thought had died long ago. To Sparky's delight, the rest of the day is filled with activities that every dog lives for. Dennis gives her food, games, and, most important, companionship.

Sparky chases the football that she has seen Dennis play with so many times before from across the street, locked away in her prison. She enjoys the hardness of it, the red color, the squeak that emanates from it every time she tightens her jaws. She darts back and forth across the yard, completely oblivious to her surroundings. The pair of legs she runs into brings her down very quickly from her ecstasy.

"Well, what have we here?" says the man's voice. In a fit of panic, Sparky darts through the man's legs and under the porch.

"Sparky! No!" cries Dennis.

"Hey get back here!" booms the man's powerful voice.

"Dad, what's going on?" asks the daughter stepping outside.

"Dennis was playing with another dog. It ran under the porch."

"Really?"

"Yeah. Can you get me the phone? I think this may be the dog that's missing from across the street."

Dennis slips under the porch and finds Sparky trembling uncontrollably. "You have to leave," he says.

"What? Why?" Sparky cries.

"They saw you come under the porch. They know you're here. You have to find another place to go."

"No, I won't go back! I can't go back there!" Sparky's voice gets louder and louder and her trembling somehow increases.

"I'm not saying to go back. I'm just saying to leave here," says Dennis.

"Where am I supposed to go?"

"I don't know! Anywhere else! Get a grip!" Dennis peeks out into the yard and sees that his owners have returned inside. "You have to make a run for it."

Sparky starts to leave but turns briefly towards Dennis. "Thank you so much. For everything." Her eyes fill with tears and she gives Dennis a kiss on the cheek.

She runs into the yard and towards the street. Dennis follows her out from under the porch but makes a turn for the house. He runs inside, and Sparky is left alone. She walks along the sidewalk, looking for an opening in the hedges lining the other yards. It isn't long before she hears Dennis's voice calling out to her in the distance.

"Sparky! Hide! They're outside looking for you!"
Sparky spins in circles with no clue as to where she could hide. Seeing nothing else, she throws herself into a pile of leaves on the side of the road. She lays low in the pile, and she can only hear their voices as they hunt for her. "Which way did she go?" "I don't know." "Did she go into someone else's yard?" "Maybe she went back to her house."

Dennis's heart races as he watches the pursuit. He can barely see the pile of leaves Sparky is hiding in without leaning and feeling the electrical pulse move through his body. That's it, Sparky. Just lay low a little while longer. Dennis can't keep his paws on the ground as the excitement of the chase persists. He runs towards the other side of the yard to release some energy. He barely makes it halfway across the yard when he hears a loud squeal, followed by screeching brakes. Dennis runs back to the edge of the yard and looks towards the pile of leaves. The leaves are scattered across the street. Dennis waits a few moments for Sparky to lift her head up. He waits for her to run. But nothing. Not a sound. No movement. Nothing. Dennis gets dizzy as the world starts to spin with Sparky's lifeless body at the center of the vortex.

Passion

Orchestrates

Enlightenment

Maximizing

Symbolism

EXPERIENCE

INSIDE

VERSES

<u>Search For A Subject...</u>

Whether you share short stories, knit novels, or compose poetry, you are constantly in search of a subject. Where do you find your inspiration? Where do you search for the sanity that is the focus of your piece? The challenge usually is finding something, someone, or some essence worthy enough to place on paper so that the goodness spills over the page into the minds and hearts of your readers.

Look for things with which you are comfortable. Seek familiar items and start with the small details, working your way through the larger ones. If you happen across those old mittens, that crumpled up hat, or the too-small-to-even-think-of-trying-on jeans, reflect on the impact they had on your life. Each has its own story. Each has its own sense of inspiration. If those are not the source, keep looking.

Look through past writings. If you have other stories or poems, search for common themes among them. If you explored only one concept in depth, pull out the others. If you wrote about your favorite pair of sneakers and focused on the soles of the shoes, write this time on the laces and how they made their way to the next pair.

Talk with others. The conversations alone will provide enough topics for a well-crafted poem let alone a random short story. If you have numerous conversations with an individual, a novel is underway. Their stories become your inspiration.

Of course, if none of these methods are not successful, you can seek out the classics and other stories...or, perhaps, take a look at the poems on the following pages.

<u>Early Mornings</u>

Early Mornings Torment me so
Why my kids do this to me I do not know

The begging the screaming – how could this be?
Oh wait that's not the kids...its me.

"Cherish these times, they grow so fast"
Really, than why do I feel that this just lasts and lasts

So now I'll return to my life of not so perfect tranquility
as I try to compose myself to deal with the day with a certain civility

Or maybe I'll go back to bed...

Teri A. Murray

Cole Ridge Poem

Blythe gale,
Peasants to hail,
Why canst thou fling free?
Soar over the churning sea in wild ecstasy?
Must you always salt my soars?
Bitter struggle tasted by scores
Inflicted by you, the curses rebound
Upon the shipwrecked Sound
Enslaving master and taskman alike
Oh, wild spirit, why not burst the dike
And fly home?
To roam
Frree

Joy Sheppard

<u>Core</u>

Apple
Below scarlet skin,
White flesh within,
Black bugs in snow,
Buried cold, slow
Apple seeds
Sift in and out of sleep.
Secrets unravel in the sand of dreams
So she must listen,
All the way to the center of things,
Here is where the silence rings,
The hollow shell of discarded cores.

Suzanne Grenoble

Watch

My girl asks Mommy what's the time? and I say
Time to sled into a snowpile, play
Make believe or cookie cop or
End the day leisurely bathing with
Unimaginable legions of friends
What time is it Mommy when the Big Hand touches twelve?
Time to stand up tall, to bat,
Stretch out long
Like a cat:
Mommy, the Big Hand is on the nine,
And the little hand is on the twelve, Mommy
Can I call someone? anyone, to tell them the time
And I say it's late but I wonder
Can I teach you
Do I reach you
Can I wish for you
Trying to rush you from bath to bed but then
Stories drag out the decision
And the light stays on
And what time will it be
When I stop asking and forget that I ever did ask, and then
Ask while you write this, why are you writing this? And
The mother raises her eyes to her beloved to
Tell her how she looked
Asleep, oval face and long brown hair
Like a fallen angel, streaming dark across the white pillow

Suzanne Grenoble

Lemon

Sea surge sluicing
Salt Citrus
Over the tongue
Pale seeds
Like transparent pebbles,
Slipslide longways,
Settling in sea algae–
Cool dark underworld green down.
Upsideways,
Yellow-bright sun pinwheels on high,
Over our celadon haven for nests.

Suzanne Grenoble

The Collapse of Summer

Trees on the steep hillside
across the river will peak
within the next few days,
and if things follow precedent,
shed their impossible colors
soon after.
The zinnias did not mean
to let themselves get so shabby.
The old gray groundhog waddles
through the cosmos, fat and sleepy.
The children we named after purple
flowers have fled the house.
Our own bodies give in
to gravity more each day,
our bones slowly emerging.
We really used to be something,
didn't we?

Timothy Russell

Selected Poems

They whirled and flurried from the sky.
They came to me in the middle of the night,
some silently, some clumsily bumping into things.
They stuck their tongues in my mouth.
Some slunk along the edge of the river bank
like feral cats. Some ran ahead of me
like those bumpkins in Pamplona.
They flicked their beautiful tail feathers.
They took things personally and sulked or pouted.
They undressed and they got dressed.
They spoke to strangers and took up with them.
Some recovered from one trauma or another.
Some did not. One saved somebody's life.
They fed me. They traveled with me.
They ventured out of the woods
and nibbled dead meat beside the highway.
They whispered in my good ear.
They scuttled down the street
behind cars and muscular pickups.
They got taken in by shysters.
Some went off somewhere to find themselves.
They danced around in skimpy outfits.
Some slowly became themselves
as if they had no idea what else to do.

Timothy Russell

The Fifty Things Wrong With This Picture

None of this will hasten
or delay that dazzling flash
astonishingly brief on the horizon.
Some of these children have never seen
a river or an orchard or a pea pod
before today. Poppies and impatiens
that make you think "cinnamon"
instead of "cinnabar" perhaps
are in simultaneous bloom
with tiger lilies and chicory
along the road and bachelor buttons
and clematis near the porch.
The children are without dread.
They investigate every crevice
for the golden apples they've heard
about. Only this morning
a man in khaki drove a green tractor
through "that protected section
yonder" beyond which coal is being stripped.
Two starlings chase a sparrow
veering crazily but not dropping
the bread crust from its beak.
Not one detail here depends
on any other, not even the boy
in the chocolate and lemon polo shirt
about to discover a handful of bees.

Timothy Russell

Bitter Awareness

What is a dream?
The word dream is scrumptious,
Like the cotton candy held in the palm of your hand,
Realistic and loud,
Like the sticky situation if held to long,
Self knowledge weighing on you like a twenty-eight pound brick dropped from the sky,
Landing in the palm of your hands,
Preservation, the key to the long roads you'll take,
Preparing yourself for what may or may not be,
Most satisfying to the mind like a cold winter's day and a cup of hot chocolate,
Your future of life, or the death of your dignity,
Your goals set before you like a steaming brownie with a perfectly round scoop of vanilla ice cream on top, most delicious when reached for, your dream!

Jamie Lynn Waters

Moving On

There comes a point in life when we all grow up
The loss of innocence,
Promises,
Heartbreaks,
Loss of loved ones,
High school,
Graduation,
It's all a part of life,
Some may experience more than others but it's what makes you, you
Don't lose your morals and faith for the pleasure of others,
Keep your ground and hold your head high,
Show people you can be who you want to be and still succeed,
Sometimes there will be a fork in the road,
Take the path in which you feel you will succeed because if worse comes to worst
There's always construction, you can make it back on that path of triumph,
It's never too late,
You'll learn from your mistakes and become more cautious as you continue on the path of life.

Jamie Lynn Waters

Sickness

Sickness is a sad thing,
Watching the color fade from your face,
Wondering how your yesterdays are,
Did you live it to the fullest,
Or was it just a mistake, regret, or nothing at all,
It could be today,
It could be tomorrow,
I'm not looking for the sorrow,
But if there never comes a tomorrow,
I want you to be satisfied with the life you lived,
Even though you still hold so much life,
It's slowly slipping from you,
Somewhere out there, there is more to life for you,
Even though I prepare myself,
I'll never be ready,
I got one brother and preparation will never be enough for that day,
Although words go unspoken amongst us,
I hope you know that there is a plan for you,
And if it be that you go before you want to,
You'll forever hold a place in my heart,
The memories left will keep us connected,
And the life you left here will know your legacy.

Jamie Lynn Waters

I forget...Is it Naptime?

I woke up early...too early...
Did I sleep OK?
I forget...
Is it naptime?
I wanted snacks and more cereal...more cereal...
Did we eat breakfast?
I forget...
Is it naptime?
I didn't eat my lunch...yucky lunch...
Did we have food?
I forget...
Is it naptime?
I want to go swimming...too hot...
Do we have a pool?
I forget...
Is it naptime?
I want ice cream for dinner...chocolate ice cream...
Did we buy cones?
I forget...
Is it naptime?
Chicken again...yucky chicken...
Do we have macaroni?
I forget...
Is it naptime?
I want three books before bed...not two...
Have we read these?
Oh, I forgot...
We missed naptime.

John E. Murray, III

INSPIRED

WITHIN

VERSES

Praise Your Muse...

A special relationship deserves to be appreciated and admired. A spouse or significant individual should be told how special they are to you and in your life. Reflect on the happiness they bring. Encourage your muse to show through the relationship and into a being all its own.

To aid in the reflection found within the mirror of your soul, research the great works and sonnets of the classic romantics. Work to develop a style that shares is shared with your romantic counterpart and your inner muse. Explore how strong your connection has become. Explain how important the shared togetherness is. Encourage the love you share to make its way onto a blank page or screen.

When you write, don't anticipate how long your gaze lingers. Keep it intense, and encourage the surges of palpitations and emotion. Let your thoughts, emotions, and ideas linger a slight bit longer to demonstrate your appreciate and connection to your inspiration.

The poems that follow delve into some of those depths. Determine where your muse will lead you.

<u>Wondrous Happiness</u>

Love is a great journey, especially when you make it with your soulmate with whom your share a wondrous happiness...

My heart alone can not sustain this wondrous happiness,
But, together alone, the inner greatness may grow,
And emotions sealed long ago, will continue to show.
Stay with me as we share this special journey,
For then the true intensity we may see.
As we tread forward into the future we create,
Let this bond we make test the depths of fate.
Our love will undoubtedly blossom into a full and beautiful flower,
Until then, let us be immersed in the pulsing power
Of the sustained togetherness and wondrous happiness.

John E. Murray, III

The Night Was Made For Romance

The night was made for romance.
In the night our two hearts dance.
Under the stars our lips touch.
In the garden your embrace means so much.
The night was made for love.
Our hearts cooing like a white dove.
Your eyes sparkling like diamonds so white.
I love you darling with all my might.
The night was made for caring and trust.
And darling, God made this night for us.

Our Love

As long as there is love, I will cherish you.
As long as there is life, I will love you.
As long as the stars shine above, I will want you.
As long as there are waves in the ocean, I will need you.
As long as there is heaven above, there will always be our love.

Only Love

Love can sometimes be fresh.
Love can sometimes be new.
Love can sometimes make you happy.
And sometimes make you blue.
Love is the light that radiates from your eyes.
Love is your image floating in the skies.

Love is true.
And darling, the only love for me is you.

Lamar Cole

108

My Lover, My Friend

Butterflies, goose bumps, even chills,
When I'm with you that's how I feel.
Holding you tight oh so close,
Being a part of your life is what I love the most.
My eyes sparkle, my face glows,
How much you mean to me you'll never know.
I love being a part of your world,
Everyday I feel like the luckiest girl.
You're my man, my best friend,
The bond we have is impossible to end.
Deep thoughts, secrets told,
Sharing these feelings will never get old.
Being apart for a day feels like years,
You have helped me overcome my fears.
I love you like there's no tomorrow,
Where ever you go I'll follow.
You're my soul mate, my better half,
You always know how to make me laugh.
Each fight made us who we are today,
The bond is stronger now nothing can stand in our way.
Thank you for loving me and everything you do,
But mostly thank you for being you.

Crystal Robin Rose

So Lost

When your away
My eyes cry
Tiny little tears
On my pillow
I feel so alone
When your not
Here
I wish you
Would come back
Home
Where you need
To be
Because I feel
So Lost
Without you

Michele Lee Moyer

<u>Who Are You?</u>

Sometimes I question myself
When I begin to do things, I never done before
Is this maturity, am I bettering myself
Or is this post teen peer pressure where I following a flock
Who are you?
Sometimes you have to ask
Because people have motives
What are yours?
Is it to close every door left open by our ancestors?
Or, is it to break the frame
So that more people can have the opportunity to break free
From self arresting chains
Don't confuse it, if you don't use it you definitely lose it
So when will you change
From using words for gossip to creating beautiful stories
Filled with your soul and provide it
To other people as a real life object or testament
Of fall down, get back up, keep trying
Now tell me, who are you?
Are you the pen that continue to poison our history
With ignorance, disloyalty and murder
Or were you just the instrument of crime to put us down further
Well, now is the your time to stand for something
Other then your own selfish needs of fulfillment
You can become the pen that will one day write our future
Therefore, today I ask who are you?

Damien Livingston

Perfect Man

Just foolish, thinking I can be a perfect man
Look at my face masked wit incorrect thoughts
Or this body of mine... that has been bathed in self ignorance
Listen to the words I speak from the depth of my mouth that are not
genuine but are instead dishonest and misleading
Or the loss look in my eyes... smothered with life's tragedies
I'm just foolish, for there is only one who's perfect
Why do I ache for approval from relatives and friends ..., or, lust for
acceptance from foreign faces
Where did I misplace my self respect, or bury my integrity
What would make me sacrifice my inner potency, for shame and guilt
Most times I feel lost in this abandoned house known as my Life
Unsheltered from self-hatred, adverse depression and redundant let
downs
Yet, I find myself looking for a savior
Looking for someone to feel sorry for me
Yearning for compassion..., starving for unbeneficial pity
Chasing a mirage of a Perfect man
Left me scorn, drowning in a sea of hatred
For I forgot to accept myself, forgot to believe in myself... but most of
all I forgot to love myself
I forgot to tell myself that as long as I give it my all

I'm am perfect, perfectly me as I can be

Damien Livingston

ENGAGE

WITH

VERSES

__Read, Then Write...__

So, you are thinking of writing that great novel…the intense short story…or, that inspirational poem…You have your setting, your subject, your time…Have you remembered to read other writings like yours? Reading stories, poems, and sentences like you wish to write brings you closer to the words and audience with which you are trying to connect. Visit your local book stores, check out online booksellers, stop by your local library, or dust off one of those old volumes on your shelves. Don't just read the newspaper or the catchy headline magazines. These items will just give you words not necessarily the right words for your characters or for your readers.

Each book on writing should coming with a warning "Do not try this on your own…" because, you don't have to…many others have been there before you. Many others are there with you now. Read the writing of others before, during, and after you write. Think of the paths the authors of your favorite poems, stories, and books took to bring you into their world.

Just as the writers in this section have done, follow your own guide and bring your story or poem along, so that your muse may clear away the cobwebs from the map that is being redrawn for your own tale…

It is a long...long...long day...

Today...today, I say
Was, in fact, a long, long, long day...
The fact is there
And, everywhere...
As it the solstice is here.
When did this sneak up on us?
When did we get into this rush?
Enjoy the light...
Refuse the night...
Reach for the stars
If you can stay awake...
Leave the bugs in the jars
From yesterday
For they will be out too late.
Enjoy, rejoice, and celebrate
This summer solstice date.

John E. Murray, III

The Machine: Time Driven

Metal pieces,
The ocean breeze,
An open door,
As if to say, "Hello."
The blood of man.
Stood up there,
And through his lips spoke to the world,
But throught the world is where his words now lay scattered.
Time passes by,
An old man died,
But not soon to be forgotten.
For in this man,
There was no fear,
To take a stand and to be heard.

Cathy P. Staley

<u>Ad Finem</u>

Today is the same as yesterday.
Tomorrow will be the same as today.
Misery pushes open the door of desperation.
A lull descends upon demeanor, and hopes quickly dissipate.
Soon becomes an afterthought.
Time passes.
Tomorrows come, and yesterdays pass with no change in incident.
Time is no friend of irrevocable circumstance.
Spirit is broken, and all becomes submissive.
Only to immortalize that which is influential.
It's this time, all times, all ways. Ad finem.
To the end.

Jody McMaster

Interpretations

I cant suppress all these memories. Why would I try?
The past, like a songbird perched matter-of-factly on my window sill.
Not to be neglected. Passed down, recorded, each one.
On blank pages are penned an account of my life.
Etched on my brain for eternity.
Each one so vivid, like a beacon in the darkest of night.
They are replayed on a stage set in my mind.
I can return again and again to each scene, or not. Prolonged or fleeting; or not at all.
I am the keeper of these abstract thoughts.
There is no moderation. Only anything and everything.
Like sacred writings, I will read until my senses are full.
Until each perception has been nurtured,
all my impressions have been completely and entirely saturated,
every sensation has been manipulated absolutely.
They will continue on their voyage. There is no lull.
They peak, and my intellect becomes intoxicated. They have come to anchor now.
A hushed calm occupies my will. All reflection recedes.
Back to the recesses of my intellect. But only for a brief intermission.
Nestled among exaggerations, secrets, and misinterpretations.

Jody McMaster

Life is Rough

Life is rough
It has its roads
Some are hard
That's a fact that I will always know
You see kids getting beaten
It is not a lie
For every night that I stayed up praying and wishing to die
Its sad
Yes I know that
But you have to understand that I am not bad
I love the Adirondack youth lodge
And I love the people in it
Its the best place to ever live at
So thanks guys for all the help

Kaylee Lynn Gates

<u>Holocaust</u>

The bluebird chirps of love tonight
As two form one in close embrace.
Love's power strains beyond all might
To ease the ache of life's hard race.
Vain words of hope he breathes this hour;
She sobs the more as daybreak comes.
A tyrant grasps them in his power,
And death will make them all succumb.
Hadassah wept, so Haman dies—
A consequence of God-heard prayer.
Yet no redeemer will arise
To save the sons of Isaac's heir.
The couple clings for one last time.
Cold Auschwitz's darkness lurks in sight
As now approach death's gas and lime.
The bird's song dies with dawn's first light.

Hannah Ruth Steadman

For What I Know

For what I know and what I'll be
I will remember I was he
Who knew of what was in the sea,
For know I this and know I well
That I was on the wall, then fell.
And had you seen me stumble on
When night encountered what was dawn
Then know I this and know I well
That though I stumbled, though I fell,
I will remember I was he
Who knew when what was known of me.
For though the dark descends to claim
The very mention of a name,
I will remember I am he
Who sees the dark fall in the sea.
For battles rage and this I know-
That though I know not what you know,
Still I am here throughout the year
To settle down when I will fear.
And should a day proclaim me dead,
Still I remember what was said
When I remember what was bled
When I remember I was dead.

Frank Kilbourn

Changing Times

Seasons change from summer to fall
Winter coming with an early frost
Plants start to shrievel up and turn brown
Grass soon turns into hay
Trees begin to lose all the leaves
Which turned such pretty colors in the fall.
People grow and change year to year
A baby learns its first word
Two new parents so brilliantly excited
A young boy learns to ride his bike
Like everything does in the cycle of life
People may grow, things may change
We can choose to accept it or run scared

Life is meant to be lived to the fullest

The weather might not all be sunny
You might not always wear a smile

Laughter may never come

Connections may be lost between good friends

In the end, one thing is constant
That is which we call, love.

Courtney Lyn Blystone

REACHING

INTO YOUR

VERSES

Find Your Time and Write…

When the muse arrives, make sure you have something on which to capture at least the falling remnants of your inner voice…a notepad, a napkin, or your text, web, or email-enabled phone. Don't lose the muse moment simply because you didn't expect it. If you are in a situation where you can't crank out thousands of words, capture the thoughts, the ideas, a handful of words and phrases so that you can return to them when you have the time.

If you are one of those fortunate individuals, who have realized that your muse arrives each morning at 8 AM sharp and you have reorganized your schedule to accommodate the muse moments, take that first breathe to appreciate the inspiration and write where it takes you. Don't stop, don't hesitate. Don't question. Just write. If you pause to ask questions, that coordinated time will be less productive, and you may also stop the time all together. It is as if you had a guest to your home and interrupted him/her every time he/she decided to say something. That would probably make for shorter, less frequent visits and relationships.

Explore your thoughts the best way you know how. The award-winning poems in this section encourage a new standard and help set the scope of what you may write about in your next muse moment.

<u>Wanting to Become Me</u>

Imagine my inner walls crumbling,
Dreaming the impossible,
Unrefined thinking like a child's world,
I am already great,
And my greatest wish is to become me.

I'm infected with reality,
Or at least its image,
And though I don't care for its false hope,
I'm struggling to break its bind,
For it happens daily.

I've been motivated to change,
Not myself, by the ways of myself,
To step slightly into the shoes of destiny,
It's a perfect fit, my feet, the shoes, destiny,
Why won't I wear the shoes?

Am I afraid of greatness?
To seek out and have the impact I know I am capable of achieving,
If I am already great,
The only thing that should stay impossible,
Is holding tight to the smallness of comfort.

The walls are crumbling,
Dreaming is inevitable,
We are all children learning and growing,
We are all great,
It is my turn now to become me.

Skyler Wolf Jones

An Ending Of A Similar Kind

I looked into your eyes and saw mine;

The countenance on your face sent me traveling back in time;

The love that poured from your heart reminded me of another;

It was the same love I had shared with my mother;

On a hot, muggy, August morn my mother went away;

My age was young and tender, but I can still clearly remember that day

I woke to a world that suddenly felt enormously big and round;

And I, like the tiniest ant, now seemed to small to ever be found;

I wondered how or if I would again have a place where I belong;

For my mother was gone, my life no longer had its song;

Then I woke early one magnificent morn to a brand new world;

One filled with hopes and dream meant just for this little girl;

So, I dug in my heels and went searching for all I could discover;

Eager to see what possibilities lay ahead, each I wanted to uncover;

The road I traveled surely was not easy;

There were many dips twists bumps and curves;

Many times I nearly quit, many times I nearly lost my nerves during those dark scary moments when it didn't feel much like i was winning;

But with an iron will and soul full of hope, I leaped in and sent myself spinning on a journey with no light, no map, not direction sign

Just sheer determination to find the life destined to be mine;

Though I'm much older, there still remains much more work to, and on the very top of my list was to write this poem just for you;

To leave a message that I pray you're always keep close in mind;

For as you travel your life's journey, you may face a string of endless struggles;

But if you refuse to give up, refuse to quit each and every time;

One bright early morn, you too, will rise beneath a sea of stars to find that we not only share a story with a familiar beginning, but with an Ending Of A Similar Kind.

E.D. Arrington

Ship of Gold

My heart is the captain for a ship of gold
Our mission is something special to behold
Together, my boat and I span the high seas
We ride through the turmoil with the greatest ease
Clear skies form to greet us and welcome our cause
There's no hesitation found to bring us pause
So onward we go, though the dawn turns to night
Our destination firmly fixed in our sight.
Alas, we've seen struggles through which some would fail
But, my ship and I are destined to prevail
No rock 'neath the surface or force from a wave
Could make us believe our course is not to save
My ship and I know what we can and can't take
Such trust and assurance leaves calm in its wake
When the stars appear, come the moon's brilliant glow
Toward our final port call, my ship and I go.
My heart is the captain for a ship of gold
Yet, found in the cargo, there's something quite old
A masterpiece which has lived through tests of time
A gift for the ages, still well in its prime
Some call it a blessing, reserved for a few
Yet, when we dock portside, I'll give it to you
The "gold" in my cargo is love, evermore
My dear, I will see you when I reach the shore.

Jill Eisnaugle

The Love You Share

May your love be like the ocean
Ever peaceful and carefree
May your fondness and devotion
Last throughout eternity
May your dreams be like a feather
Made to float upon the air
As you spend this life together
Bound within the love you share.

May your love be like a beacon
Serving as your blessed guide
May your spirit never weaken
As you pass each test in stride
May your memories be measured
By the years that you shall see
And the tidings ever treasured
That shall form your legacy.

May your love be like the glory
In the sun's rich morning rays
May your visions write a story
To rest in your hearts, always
So that every day you borrow
Shall be free from all despair
As you face each new tomorrow
Bound within the love you share.

Jill Eisnaugle

A Newborn Child

A newborn child with eyes so bright
You fill the world with much delight
Your heart is kind; your smile is sweet
You are a joy to those you meet
Formed in the palm of God's own hand
Your destiny appears quite grand
Although, your path is just begun

Your future shines, just like the sun.
As moments pass, your soul will grow
To learn things that you did not know
You'll rise above; you'll make mistakes
You'll fall in love; your heart will break
Yet, through it all, you will remain
A link within your family's chain
Whose bond shall strengthen over time
Despite the mountains you must climb.

A newborn child with eyes so bright
You are, indeed, a wondrous sight
Your skin is soft; your features small
But, you are loved by one and all
I know tears fell from cherubs' eyes
As they embraced you with goodbyes
Before you flew from high above
To grace us with God's gift of love.

Jill Eisnaugle

Snowflake

The human heart is like a snowflake
With compassion, ever free
As each moment we are awake
We are bound in empathy
When we join to help a neighbor
Whose needs surpass our own
We shall find our gift of labor
Is the greatest glory known.

The gifts we give to another
Once our lives link, hand in hand
Are pleasures, like nothing other
When our deeds blanket the land
Just as the sunlight of winter
Often shines a lasting glow
Our hearts beam, when last we enter
Hope where once pain had bestowed.

These snowflakes are quite distinctive
But their common ground is clear
Their ambitions are instinctive
From the moment they appear
While solo, their means are shallow
When united, they shall be
Pristine splendor, ever hallowed
With glamour for all to see.

The human heart is like a snowflake
Whose compassion freely flows
Each moment when we are awake
Like a drift destined to grow
For despite life's squally weather
Much promise can be instilled
When our hearts unite together
 In a blanket of goodwill.

Jill Eisnaugle

Open Range

He traveled 'cross the open range
No shirt upon his back
Longing to reach outer LaGrange
Before the sky turned black
A cattleman since birth, it seemed
He lived the herdsman's life
But, late at night, the cowboy dreamed
Of his children and wife.

His family had placed its roots
Along the river bend
But, none could take his western boots
When daylight reached its end
His heart was tethered to the trail
'tis where his life was blessed
He worked the landscape, without fail
Driving the livestock west.

The years had always been a friend
But, time was wearing thin
He knew he should let others tend
The cattle and the gin
Ten years before, he'd made a pledge
Before he went to sleep
And, as he stood at Red Oak Ledge
He prayed his soul to keep.

"Lord, take the reins from these two hands
And let the cattle roam
I've seen the last of these fine lands

'tis time that I go home
My days upon the trail are through
I've reached the setting sun
So, with this prayer, I bid adieu
I've left too much undone."

"I'm going home to hold my wife
Beside the firelight
I'll share tales of the herding life
With my kids, every night
I thank you for these years, I've known
Yet, I must step aside
I'm tired of days spent alone
But, grateful for the ride!"

Those final words came from the heart
And were etched in the clay
Since the life and he did depart
That late September day
The souls who knew the herdsman well
Swear that the stars above
Shone brightly o'er his little dell
Once he embraced his love.

Jill Eisnaugle

<u>Live, Laugh, Love</u>

May every dream be yours to keep
May every joy be near
May every hour without sleep
Be one of warmth and cheer
May every beat within your heart
Be blessed with much to give
So, each path is a work of art
Each day that you shall live.

May every smile upon your face
And every childish grin
Be filled with memories to embrace
As if you're young again
May each sunrise bring cause to view
Life's humor for its pleasure
So, each path you choose to pursue
Yields laughter beyond measure.

May every vision in your eyes
Be for those you hold dear
May you know only brilliant skies
Where shooting stars appear
And with each shooting star, I pray
Your hopes are heard, above
So, every path to come your way
Is paved in lasting love.

Jill Eisnaugle

<u>The Christmas Angel</u>

One long, lost and solemn winter, several years ago, it seems,
A boy stood beside a forest, with only his hopes and dreams.
As he peered beyond the tree line, only darkness did he find;
Then, a certain Christmas marvel came before his lonely mind.
From the sky above, a clearing showed a silhouette of peace,
Brightened by the brilliant starlight, shining o'er the snowy fleece.
On the ground, a tiny angel, traced upon the frozen land,
Taught the boy of Christmas blessings and the gifts at his command.

The boy stood lost in amazement, awed by the sight 'fore his eyes;
Then, he peered upon the Heavens and much to his own surprise,
Suddenly, the tree limbs parted to reveal a golden hue,
And a sign that read, *"This season is the time when dreams come true."*
The boy returned to the angel, traced upon the winter's snow,
His mind filled with Christmas wonder and his heart, at last, aglow.
With a newfound sense of comfort and a restored sense of joy,
Stood a child, strong and courageous, where once had been a lonely boy.

One long, lost and solemn winter, several years ago, it seems,
A boy stood beside a forest and realized his hopes and dreams.
Each was found within the spirit of the Christmas holiday,
And the "season made for dreaming" is alive and well, today.
So remember as you gather, with your friends and family near,
The many reasons you are humbled by this treasured season's cheer.
My very best to you, this Christmas; may your heart be filled with love,
And your dreams be blessed by angels, traced by God's own hand, above.

Jill Eisnaugle

The Pearl

Upon the seashore lies a pearl; indeed, a priceless sight
A beautiful creation, enclosed in an oyster's might
A small, yet cherished fortune etched so proudly on display
A sign of tender love to last forever and a day
The pearl is fashioned over time, grown far beneath the earth
A breathtaking expression of true miracles and worth
A grain of sand within a shell; this pearl in life shall yield
A testament of courage and God's destiny revealed.

Just like the pearl upon the shore, your love has spanned the years
You've formed a wealth of hopes and dreams, through hard work and
through tears
Your lives have grown stronger and surer, as you've forged ahead
With love remaining certain, as it was the day you wed
Your bond has fashioned over time and brought tremendous pleasure
A wonderful example that such love is quite a treasure
Your two lives joined, embraced as one united grain of sand
Your marriage is a blessing, sanctified by God's command

The moment when your two hearts met, your pearl readied for life
'twas touched by faith and smoothed by hope 'til you were man and
wife
Then on the day your lives were one, your fond pearl came to be
A sign of tender love to reign throughout eternity
The years have passed and your pearl is perfect and flawless, still
Your hearts are true, your marriage strong; indeed, this is God's will
This day, your lives have vowed, once more, to share a lifetime through
You've reaffirmed the hopes and dreams you've valued since I do.

I pray that you shall live in love until your setting sun

I pray your hearts shall remain bound, never to be undone
I pray that you shall always know the beauty in God's favor
That every day your lives shall see is something you will savor
Most of all, I pray that you will look back and remember
The years you've known and goals you've shared, since your love was an ember
The romance and the blessings lived and those yet to unfurl
As you go forth, as man and wife, with your love's sacred pearl.

Jill Eisnaugle

__Breast Cancer Survivor's Prayer__

Dear Lord, You've done so much for me
Thank You with all my soul
But, I've something to ask of thee
Needing Your grand control
I've waged this battle and I've won
Yet, others battle still
For some, their journey's just begun
Please guide each in Your will.

I've walked this road; I've felt each bump
I have conquered Your test
I've grown much wiser, since the lump
Located in my breast
I see the world much differently
I pray others will, too
So many fight audaciously
Lord, help to see them through.

Dear Lord, I ask with all my heart
Please touch these special lives
Bless them with courage from the start
Bring hope into their eyes
Let their hope shine a hallowed light
That burns forevermore
To honor their spirited fight
And our dreams for a cure.

Jill Eisnaugle

__Good Morning__

Good morning, as you rise and shine
Another day in life is here
The hour has come to redefine
Your journey 'cross the wild frontier
Beneath a sky, in cobalt hue
You'll stroll along your merry route
While I hope all the best for you
As you continue your pursuit.

Good morning, as the moonlight fades
And you begin your daily chores
The dawn is bright; open the shades
Then, dream until each wish is yours
Throughout the day, you'll move in stride
As I hold your heart in each prayer
Every time that you look outside
You'll know that I am waiting there.

Good morning, as you greet the world
Once more, your life begins anew
A fresh beginning has unfurled
And brought your goals within your view
While you seek to embrace your dreams
I'll wish you well, 'til day is done
I'll keep you safe, beneath my beams
Have a great day! Regards, the sun.

Jill Eisnaugle

__Timeless Tales...__

When tales do we tell,

Inside, meaning must dwell.

While ideas circle, collide, and swirl,

To select one insightful pearl,

We lightly linger and weave

Through intensities each believe.

Excitement mounts until the expected end,

As each delicate page we do bend.

In between can be found,

Delightful descriptions and rich details abound.

A truly timeless tale found within

Answers perfectly how and where to begin.

John E. Murray, III